CALI

WRITTEN BY

DEBORAH FRAZIER

Acknowledgements

I want to give honor to my Heavenly Father who is known as "I AM THAT I AM "THANK YOU FATHER "AND TO His Son my Lord and Savior JESUS CHRIST.
This book is dedicated to my mother, Pauline Alston Butler. She still inspires me even through her death "I love you mommy".

To my daughter's Pauletta, Destiny, Shannon and my son in-law Jimmy Clanton the third I love all of you and I Hope you will be proud of me. Remember whatever you say, that you're going to do or wanting to do, "do it".

To my grandchildren Kyra, Tymir and Gregory Jr., khamilah, Jimmy the forth and my Great Grand Adam. I am expecting great thing out of all of you.

To my sisters and brother Rita, Gay and Bridgett, Linwood Jr I love you and I am still here.

To my cousins, nieces and nephews, I am so happy to see all of you doing so well.

To my friends who have stuck with me, with your encouraging words has helped me to keep Cali alive. "Thank you."

Special Thanks

Thanks, to Mr. Tyler Perry for his face book inspirations. Especial the one called "Thank God for Closed Doors".

Thanks to my editor Ms. Kyra Usher for listening to me and giving me back my book without changing my story.

Thanks to Mr. Jimmy Clanton Jr graphic art designer and IT specialist for editing my book cover and book formatting.

Thanks to a very special neighbor Allen who looks out for me. After a couple of home issues, he makes it bearable to come home and he never asks for anything in return you are appreciated more than you know.

*More books to come

This story was based on public in formation, that children are being changed from one sex to another also called Gender Change. The people involved are Doctors and Parents they're basing their decision on the fact that the children are young enough to adapt to the changes. However there is some that have fallen thru the cracks and their bodies and mind cannot put the two together as one. You may hear some of them on TV shows telling us that they don't feel like they're in the right bodies, but are ignored as freaks.

****

Well the story of Cali is written on the latter none of the characters in the story are true or place of incident. It is a fictional thought in the

writer's mind to indulge the readers to at least think about the children'
that she calls the "children of change".

Contents

Chapter 1

At the dawn of a six am shift commotion fills labor and delivery; something totally different from the normal buzz of welcoming new life. Nurses were scrambling back and forth with grave looks of concern etched across their faces. From the looks of it; there was trouble with a baby. The doctor on call, Dr. Martin said he would have to talk with the parents and give them the news of their discovery. He took a deep breath while removing his gloves and threw them in the trash. Glancing haggardly towards one of the nurses; he asked her to get the father from the waiting area and take him to the room so he could meet with him and his wife. Mr. Evans; a tall decorated military man stood to his feet looking anxious and proud to finally hear word of his new born son. Following the nurse, he can't help but beam with pride as he is escorted to his wife's room.

He leans down to kiss her while asking, "Hi honey, how are you feeling?"

She replies in a very tired voice, "I'm fine, just a little nervous because of the way they rushed the baby out of the room when he was born. Is everything okay? What is it they're not telling us?"

Knowing how his wife could work herself into frenzy with worry he tried to reassure her that everything was alright by telling her they just want to check his vitals and make sure he was okay. They clinched each other's hands as they waited; holding on to each other and the reason they'd come up with. Each passing minute it took for them to bring the baby back into the room the more they began to worry. Finally hearing the door swiftly open they both glanced up excitedly; expecting to see the nurse pushing the bassinet with their bundle of joy, but instead Dr. Martin came in with a very dismal look on his face, that only heighten the parent's fears.

Pinching his nose to release the tension building there, he gathered himself to tell them news about their baby; "The baby was breathing fine and for the most part healthy..." He pauses a few seconds too long for their liking; "but he was born with an abnormality in his genitals."

Mr. Evans was the first to speak, "Um, what do you mean an abnormality in his genitals?"

Giving further explanation to an astounded couple, the doctor stated he was born with his genitals inside out. Mrs. Evans let out a scream of distress demanding to see her baby. The doctor told her she could see him but, he would have to remain in the incubator in a sterile environment.

It was as if she did not hear a word the doctor had said, she just kept screaming, "Why can't I see my baby!? What is wrong with him?!? Bring me my baby now!"

Beyond hysterical; her husband tried to calm her, but she was inconsolable and determined to get out of bed to see her son. "I have to see him! Let. Me. See. My baby!

Close to being distraught himself, Dr. Martin called for a nurse and ordered a sedative for Mrs. Evans. It took two nurses and her husband to restrain her in order to give her a shot but once she was calmed, Mr. Evans asked in a very firm voice; "Doc? Can we talk in the hallway?" Glancing back at his wife who was now sedated, he continued. "Now, tell me in detail what's going on with my son?"

Dr. Martin explained further that his son was born with his penis inside out and his testicles mangled. Because of this, he will not be able to perform as a man. Confused, Mr. Evans asked the inevitable. "Well, what are we to do?"

Dr. Martin took a moment to gauge Mr. Evans demeanor before answering. Calmly, he states we have perform, this surgery before. "He can be transformed into a girl, but as a girl she would not be able to have children."

Mr. Evans asks, "How will the rest of him function as a girl?"

The doctor answers, "She will need hormone shots and will have to be raised as a girl."

The once proud father that expected to see his first born son was left with a jilt in his heart. All of his training in combat and making strategizing decisions for his troops could not have prepared him for the choice he will have to make concerning his own son. Dr. Martin touched Mr. Evans on the shoulder as if to say, I know what you must be feeling before saying, "I'll need your decision as soon as possible on what you and your wife wants to do."

When the doctor left, Mr. Evans went back into his wife's room to find the sedative had taken affect. He decides to go down to the nursery to see his son since she was asleep. He felt kind of apprehensive. For a moment he just stood at the door of the nursery. Calling on the soldier within he entered the nursery and the nurse handed him a gown and a face mask to put on. Unsure of what he'd see; he looked at his son and saw the similarity in him. He touched his son's hand and the baby gripped his hand back and tried to open his eyes to see him. At that moment Mr. Evans cried for the first time since being a teenager. Trying to picture their son's life that lay ahead had him totally drowned in emotions. He returned to his wife's room and just sat looking at her and dreading what he had to tell her. She slept thru the night, which allowed him time to gather his thoughts of how to tell her about the decision they would have to make.

When she awoke in the morning she noticed her husband sleeping and slightly smiled. Hearing her move, he opened his eyes and quickly sat up. He didn't know what to expect since she had to be sedated over the news of their son. She asked him what was wrong because she noticed his eyes were red as if he had been crying. She had never seen her husband looking so disheveled; he was normally very neat in appearance and no matter what the situation always in control. The events of the day before slowly began to replay in her mind and she suddenly began to slowly slouch down in the bed and laid her head back on her pillow and stared at the ceiling. Mr. Evans got up from the chair to sit on the side of the bed next to his wife and held her hand. He began to tell her what Dr. Martin had explained to him concerning the condition of their son and the choice he's giving them to make.

Tears slowly trickled down her cheeks as she gasped and she placed her hands over her mouth to prevent from crying aloud. She looked at her husband mournfully before asking; "How did this happen? Was it was my fault?"

"Oh, no, honey! This had nothing to do with you." Trying to console her, continued. "It was just the way he was growing inside your body. I went to the nursery to see him. He looks just like me. I touched his hand and he gripped my finger." He said with a sad smile. "Other than his birth defect he's healthy. Would you like to see him? That may help us in making our decision, whether he should remain a boy or changed to a girl." Her husband looked at her with skepticism, as he reminded her that he knew this would be a big decision, but it had to be done with urgency. He pressed; the Doctor needs to know how to best approach this and it will be pending on our decision. Shaking her head yes , that she understood the urgency, but still not willing to say yes to her baby's surgery I just can't look at him now as a boy then make a decision to change him to a girl, I just can't do that! When I see my child it will be final, whether boy or girl. Why is it such an urgency, it's not life threatening? Can't they give us a day or two to research this?

Just as they were trying to make a decision, the grandparents came in excited to see their first grandchild. Their excitement was short lived after being told the news that he may be changed to a girl. The grand parents were uneasy and weren't afraid to make their reservations known. Never having heard of anything like this they voiced their strong opinion that if God made him a boy then they should leave him that way. Wanting them to see things from a different perspective; Mr. Evans went in to explain, "He will not be able to function as a man and if he gets married how would he please his wife?"

Still not convinced they said, "God will make away. He always does. He never makes mistakes." Mrs. Evans saw how much this was upsetting her husband. He was already questioning his feelings and now he had to deal with four more opinions. He needed to be sure that he was doing the right thing for his son and his family.

After hearing more than enough of her parents quoting bible verses, she firmly says, "Stop! Mom! She rubs her temples in frustration before continuing. "This will have to be a decision made by Mike and me. We are the ones who will have to live with whatever choice we make, so please just support us through this difficult time."

Her Dad; the first to answer, "We didn't mean to upset you honey. You're absolutely right. We'll love our grandchild no matter what, but if you are having doubt let God figure it out."

Seeing there was nothing else to say, they stand to leave. "We're going to the nursery to see the baby and then heading back home. We'll see you when you all get settled at home."

After their parents left Mike sat down in the chair and shook his head in despair. This decision was becoming too overwhelming for him. He suggested they talk with the doctor once more to be clear as what to expect if he stayed a boy or if they should make such a life altering choice to make their son a girl. When Dr. Martin came into the room this time Mrs. Evans was very much in control and ready to rationally discuss the fate of her son. The doctor explained in better detail, if he remained a boy he would not be able to function in the genital area but as girl she would not be able to have children.

Mrs. Evans asked, "With all of this modern technology why can't they do something to fix him?"

Dr. Martin shook his head with empathy as he told her, "I'm sorry if there was I wouldn't have to ask you to make such a decision. There is nothing that I know of."

Mr. Evans had heard enough and said, "Thank you Dr. Martin we will be letting you know our final decision soon."

When the doctor left, Mr. Evans threw him hands up in defeat; "Let's just change him to a girl. It seems like it would be easier for him as a girl. And if she wants kids she could always adopt. I cannot bear to think of my son not being able to perform as a man and getting teased when going to the locker room showers and the military; that is out of the question. After hearing everything her parents had to say gave way to doubt. Mrs. Evans wondered aloud, "But what if he found a wife that would love him for who he is?"

Mr. Evans agreed, "Yes, that's right what if? But think about it, he'll have a better chance in this world being a woman."

Fearful, confused, hurt, and sad all at the same time; Mrs. Evans conceded, "Mike, this will have to be your decision. I thought I could decide, but I just can't." Mike held his wife and tried to reassure her; as well as hiself; as he said, "This will work out; you'll see."

Mike called for the doctor again; this time to give him the decision . . . to change their son into a girl.

Chapter 2

After several hours of surgery the doctor finally came and told them everything went well and they now officially have a little girl. Mrs. Evans, anxious to see her baby asked she be taken down to the nursery; she was not going to take no for an answer this time around. She wanted to see for herself how "well" she was. The doubt she felt crept its way into her heart as she tried to imagine what their baby looked like; the kind of life he, now she, would now have to face. *"She; I'm going to have to get used to saying she instead of he. She's definitely not the boy we anticipated."* She thought to herself. She shoved it all into the crevices of her mind as her eyes beheld the sight of her precious baby; she couldn't hold her, only touch her tiny hand. The baby had features like her husband, but the pink blanket and hat certainly made her look like a girl. The longer she stared at this tiny person the deeper the ill feeling in her heart on whether they made the right decision, but it was too late now. She had to look forward and focus for the baby's sake. Coming up with a name fit for a boy or girl; she named their daughter Cali. After a few weeks of recovery Cali was released from the hospital with a clean bill of health; they were allowed to take their baby home.

*****

The first couple of years were pretty easy; they were able to control everything Cali did. It wasn't until she was about five years old they noticed she wanted to play with the neighborhood boys and play with boy's toys; dump trucks and action figures. She was not interested in baby dolls in any way shape or form; she would rip their heads off. Mr. Evans could no longer put Cali on his lap and cuddle with her like a father would normally do with a daughter. He didn't know if his wife began to notice or if she purposely blocked out the fact their daughter was beginning to act like the child she was born to be; a boy. He was devastated by the decision he'd made which would affect his child for the rest of her life. In hind-sight; he realized his decision was based on his selfish pride and ego. And the worst part; not once did he turn to God in prayer to ask for help in this matter. It was a harsh reality he now acknowledged that even though he changed his son's body; he did not change his mind. For the first time in his life Mr. Evans ran like a coward; he started to be home less and less; leaving his wife to take care of Cali. He re-enlisted for more years in the service and volunteered for deployments because he couldn't find the words to tell his wife because of him, they'd made a mistake.

By the time Cali was eleven she'd stopped wearing dresses; pretty much anything lacy and frilly or anything considered too girly. She would squirm in discomfort and anger whenever she had to wear dresses to church and other family functions. Sometimes throwing an all-out temper tantrum relieved her of having to wear them. It was on those days her mother would settle for a nice pair of pants, matching blouse, and dressy loafers. Her mother began to get worried since Cali was fast approaching her teenage years and all of the hormonal changes that come with it. With Mike gone on another tour of duty she went to see the doctor with her concerns regarding Cali's behavior. He tried to convince her not to worry because being she was raised as a girl; people would think she's just acting like a tom boy and he tried to further acquiesce her worries by adding how she'll grow out of it once she gets into high school. This response wasn't good enough for Mrs. Evans and she pressed him further about her approaching the years she should be starting her menstrual cycle and growing breasts.

Giving into her challenging questions; he finally suggested something he knew he'd eventually have to address; "Well, Mrs. Evans, there are hormone treatments we can begin giving her."

She replied with weariness, "And what should I tell her when I bring her here?"

Understanding her frustration he helped her concoct a half-truth by saying, "Just tell her after her last check-up we found she's slightly anemic and will need iron shot."

Releasing the breath she'd been holding; she dug herself deeper into their deception and replied, "Okay doctor. I hope that will work. Cali is highly perceptive and intelligent for his, I mean her eleven years." Even with all of the time that had passed she still found it difficult sometimes to remember to call Cali a girl. She gathered her purse and keys and walked with the gait of a defeated soul as she gathered her thoughts of how to not only explain these shots to Cali, but to Mike as well; that's if he ever decided to call.

After a night of tossing and turning and waiting on a call from her husband that never came; Mrs. Evans took Cali to see Dr. Martin for her first "iron" shot. Explaining it to Cali wasn't as hard as she'd thought it would be but she still carried that lead feeling in her gut that what she was doing was horribly worse than what they'd done already by telling people Cali was a girl. Before she could change her mind and leave, Dr. Martin came into the room where they waited. He was slightly taken aback to see how much she had grown and the boyish attire she wore only made her look more like the boy she truly was. He realized why her mother was worried and glanced apologetically at Mrs. Evans before taking a seat; at this point he was too.

He introduced himself to Cali as Dr. P; the name his adolescent patients called him. Cali didn't waste any time in asking Dr. P for confirmation of why she had to get a shot.

"So Dr. P, explain to me again exactly why I have to get this shot?"

Dr. Martin glimpsed at Mrs. Evans before responding; "You're simply getting an iron shot. We found that your iron is a little low." He hated to lie to her, but he knew she had not been told she was born a boy and the reason that led to her change they felt she was too young to handle news such as that. "I'll need to inject you in your arm muscle so go ahead and roll up one of your sleeves for me please."

Satisfied his answer matched her mother's Cali said, "Okay doc give me the shot. I need to get to school. I don't like being late for homeroom. My teacher loves to have an excuse to give us detention."

Dr. Martin carried on the conversation to distract her from the size of the needle. "Oh, it sounds like you really like school."

Cali piped up excitedly, "Yeah, it's okay. I'm on the track team and I'm even faster than the boys."

"That's awesome Cali. I was into track and field when I was in school too. What events are you in?" He asked as he wiped her upper arm with an alcohol pad.

"I'm on the relay team and the hundred yard dash." Cali expounded just before feeling the prick of the needle. The pain from it didn't last long and she was glad.

Dr. Martin tossed the syringe and then his gloves into the receptacle as he said, "Okay Cali! I'm all finished. I even have a note for you to take to school and your homeroom teacher."

As Cali headed out of the door, Dr. Martin turned to Mrs. Evans and expressed the importance in keeping Cali's appointments. She promised him she would.

*****

Cali was very athletic and would challenge the boys in just about every sport they would let her play and could beat most of them. Most of the boys accepted her as one of the guys; except for Rodney. He was one of the jocks in school with chauvinistic views thanks to his father and grandfather who didn't like girls playing boys sports. Add to that, the fact that Cali could beat them at almost all of their sports really pissed him off.

One day Cali had just finished playing basketball with her friend Kevin and as she was leaving the basketball court Rodney the jock of the school said, "Hey Cali, you should check your shorts; you might find some balls down there."

Cali walked up to him and hit him so hard she broke his jaw. The principal called Cali's home and said he needed to talk with both parents. Mrs. Evans was finally able to get in touch with her husband and demanded he come to the school with her to see about Cali. When they arrived at the principal's office Cali was called out of class. Everyone, especially Mr. Evans; were alarmed to see how much Cali was trying to fit in with the boys. Since beginning her "iron" shots two years ago now, her breasts had begun to grow of which she'd gotten into the habit of banding down every morning before school. When Mr. Evans saw how his daughter looked he dropped his head in shame; knowing the truth.

Cali could see her father was ashamed of her and that bothered her to the core. To hide her pain; she gave him attitude instead as if to say to him, "Whatever." She felt bad for her mom because she knew she normally didn't leave the house looking that way. She felt her father would think she let her go dressed the way she was so Cali quickly said before sitting down, "I'm sorry mom, my clothes are in my locker. I had track. So I just kept this on." She knew it upset her mom when she would wear her boyish attire but felt so much more comfortable.

The principal ready to move on with their meeting interjected with a bit of impatience, "You are not here because of your attire. You're here because you broke another students jaw today. Ms. Evans. You know as well as the rest of the student body we have a zero tolerance for such violence.

Cali's father interrupted; "She did what?"

The principal stiffly repeated himself and added, "There was a witness that saw the other student bullying Cali. But as you know, we do not allow fighting; instead, she should have reported this to a teacher but your daughter chose to use her fists. Personally, I was shocked to hear she had the strength to break this boys jaw." Mr. and Mrs. Evans gave each other knowing glances; not surprised, they knew why. The principal went on to say, "Cali was lucky the boy's parents did not press charges. Mainly because she was a girl, but they will be asking you to pay his doctor's bill."

Mr. Evans said and nodded in agreement, "Yes of course. Please give them my contact information and we'll get this taken care of."

The principal released Cali to her parents and gave her three days suspension from school. ON the walk to the car Mr. Evans thought about all the phone calls his wife made telling him what Cali was doing. Most of these calls were long drawn out voicemail messages he knew were meant to keep him abreast of their family lives since he was hardly home anymore. And he had ignored them because he knew he could do nothing. His son was living in a girl's body.

As they drove home Mr. Evans tried to act as if he was scolding her and asked, "Why don't you act more like a girl?"

He was surprise when she retorted, "Why do you care? It's not like you never treated me like one."

He knew he had that coming but still reiterated, "You watch that tone young lady. You're in enough trouble; don't make us turn this into home restriction too." His heart convicted him as he continued to drive. He didn't have anything left in him to scold her any further. When he pulled into the driveway he didn't make any moves to park inside of the garage; he waited for his wife and Cali to get out so he could leave. Cali bounced out of the car and made tracks towards her room to get away from everyone; her room was her solace where she could be herself closed away from the world. Mrs. Evans sat for a moment hoping for some of the connection she used to share with her husband. When none came she freed a sad sigh and reached for the door to open it.

Mr. Evans said without looking her, "I'll talk to you later."

She looked at him as if to ask, "So you're still letting me handle this alone?" He couldn't bring himself to hold her stare for long, put the car in reverse, and headed back to base. As he drove off he glanced through his rearview mirror and saw the only woman he's ever truly loved standing forlornly on the front steps still not knowing the reason he'd distanced himself. He could feel her tears follow him all the way back to his apartment on base.

Chapter 3

That night after settling in at home Cali took a shower and for the first time spent a little time examining her body in a full length mirror. Feeling self-conscious and even a bit perverted for doing so, she threw a towel over the top of the mirror because although she admired her body she didn't want to see her face connected to the body she was looking at. Cali would often cry and ask God why does she feel like this? But she never allowed anyone to see her cry, not even her mother; she always carried on as if she had things under control. Cali wanted badly to ask her father to come home, but she couldn't work up the courage to pick up the phone, dial his phone number, and risk the rejection she felt would come. She didn't know why he left them. There were some days she actually found herself with a pounding headache from trying to work it all out in her head; different scenarios of what could've driven him away from home. From what her mom had told her, they used to be so in love but ironically it wasn't until after she was born her dad "needed some space" as her mom tried to explain. Cali was happy her mother never treated her like it was her fault. She knew her mother hadn't cheated on him because she looked just like him, but whatever it was; Cali didn't have a clue. At least that's what she'd convinced herself to believe. Deep down in her heart she still had that inkling of a feeling that everything had something to do with her.

With sleep escaping her like a thief in the night, Cali lay awake in bed thinking about what her father had said to her when he'd dropped them off. He'd asked her, "Why don't you act more like a girl?" His seemingly disgust with her burned a hole in her soul; she made up her mind to work harder at being the girl her father wanted her to be. So, when she was allowed to return to school she forced herself to wear a dress. Not just any old dress, but this lilac colored, A-line dress with quarter length sleeves; that hit just below the hollow of her knees to show off the shapely legs she always kept hidden with baggy basketball shorts and long socks. She paired her dress with a pair of matching wedges that were more comfortable for her than the heels her mom tried to teach her to walk in. Wearing it made Cali feel uncomfortable as usual and completely out of place. The dress layered around her burgeoning curves in all the right places; so much so, the boys teased her relentlessly throughout the day and she thought she'd even caught a few jealous glances from some of the girls. She knew they liked her and was not trying to make her feel bad, but she was very much out of her element with the girl she was working to be. She was quiet all day and didn't participate in any sports. When she went to lunch she sat in a seat in the back of the lunch room processing her feelings.

Disturbing the funk she'd worked herself into, she heard someone ask, "Can I sit here?"

Cali never looked up from the rubbery French fries served lukewarm and too salty that day. She nonchalantly answered, "Sure, I don't care." It was a girl from one of her classes; she couldn't remember which one at the time.

She sat down with a happy plop, "Hi! My name is Meghan!"

Finally Cali looked up, "Hi, my name is. . ."

"Cali!" Meghan answered before she could finish. Continuing, "I'm in most of your classes. You usually hang with the guys so that's why I've never said anything to you." Cali stared openly, but gave no response. Meghan carried on as if there just wasn't an awkward silence and stated, "I like your dress."

Cali found her voice, "Ooh please don't remind me I have this on. I'd so prefer to have on pants right now."

Cocking her head to the side, Meghan asked, "So, why do you have it on then?"

Cali answered with a voice tinged with bitterness and sadness, "Just trying to please my dad, but I can't do this tomorrow. I'll wear some girl pants but the dress thing has to go."

Another small break of silence; just not as awkward this time, they both burst into laughter. Meghan waved her hands and shook her head in empathy as she spoke, "I've never known any girl who hates dresses as much as you do." Cali further explained her disdain for wearing dresses when she admitted to Meghan how her mother used to dress her up when she was younger and as soon as she would turn her back she would purposely be in the mud. This confession made Meghan howl with a laugh deep in her belly bringing a few stares their way in the lunch room. Neither cared about that because it was at this very moment a new unbreakable bond began to form.

From that day forward Meghan and Cali were inseparable. While their friendship budded, Meghan began to show Cali how to be a young lady, but Cali fought her every step of the way. Trying to teach her how to be more feminine with her mannerisms became somewhat of a project for Meghan. She truly wanted her friend to succeed in making amends with her dad and having him proud to call her his daughter. From wearing light make-up to helping her pick out clothing she found comfortable to wear Meghan tried her best to school her on what it meant to be a girl. Wide leg trouser pants with loose fitting blouses became her staple outfits when she wanted to dress up a bit. Cali also began to share everything with Meghan things she never told her mother. She was nervous the day she decided to confide in Meghan some things she swore she'd never tell anyone. It was a boring Saturday for them as they hung out in Cali's room listening to the radio and chatting about everything and nothing. Cali thought Meghan wouldn't want to be her friend anymore after finding out what a freakazoid she turned out to be with her whacked out thoughts and all. Much to her chagrin, she found it was freeing to finally admit to feeling like she was in the wrong body. She told Meghan how she felt like a boy on the inside and how sometimes she felt attracted to girls. Meghan cried for her friend after hearing how burdened she felt. Giving her a reassuring hug, Cali muffled into Meghan's shoulder, "But I don't act on it because I know God don't like that." Meghan allowed her friend to openly speak on the feelings that had been bottled up for too long without judging her; and for that made Cali appreciated her as her best friend all the more.

Chapter 4

The hands of time marched steadily through high school for Cali as Meghan proved to be a true friend; pretty much her only friend. She loved Meghan for never telling any secrets she'd shared with her and they grew to love each other like sisters. Cali still acted like a tom boy but Meghan simply accepted Cali for who she was. They enjoyed getting a good laugh whenever Cali would beat the pants off of the guys in any sport; she'd gotten especially great at archery. Cali, inheriting height from her dad, was beginning to get very tall for a girl, but her hormone shots were keeping her from looking too masculine. Running track helped her have nice strong legs and although her eyebrows were a bit bushy she was not a bad looking girl. In another life; she would have made a very handsome boy. Although her mother still made sure she kept her appointments with Dr. P she'd strongly mentioned how she was growing tired of going. Every appointment became more stressful for not just Cali, but her mother too. Her attitude was strenuously rude when she realized what time of the month it was for her. She couldn't understand why after taking her "iron" shots for years now her blood work still showed her to be anemic; neither Dr. P nor her mother gave her a believable explanation. Thanks to the internet she didn't exhibit any of the symptoms that warranted a monthly "iron" shot in her opinion. Her mother realized the older Cali became the harder it would be to get her take the hormone shots she needed.

*****

Cali and Meghan's senior year went by entirely too fast for them as the last day of their time in high school approached. It was no surprise they decided to attend the same college. Excited for each other, Meghan decided she would go into the field of fashion design, which made sense because she was always helping others with make-overs and dressing someone up. Cali decided to go into psychology, if nothing else to give her more insight to herself.

Once finishing college Meghan took a job as personal stylist and Cali took a position at the West Wood Hospital as a psychologist in the labor and delivery department. Her job was mainly working with mothers who were undecided whether they were keeping their baby and she also screened patients who were seen in the hospital abortion clinic. Cali was very surprised at how much she loved her job; at first she studied the field of psychology for selfish reasons trying to diagnose herself but she ended up loving it and began to earn accolades for her work. Because of her very calm and pleasant demeanor she received a lot of referrals from patients and fellow colleagues.

One day one of her co-workers wanted to know her secret at staying so calm.

Cali answered with a slight smirk because I have my own psychologist . . ." just as she began to go deeper into her answer her phone rang; it was Meghan. Happy to hear her best friend's voice Cali sang out, "I was just talking about you. Hold on a sec."

She put her hands over the phone and whispered to her co-worker, "It's my best friend Meghan. I'll finish telling you about how she's my personal psychologist later."

They both laughed as her co-worker responded, "Okay Cali, I'll see you later." She continued to laugh on her way out of the door.

When Cali resumes her conversation, Meghan asked wanting to laugh too, "What was all the laughter about?"

Cali responded, "I'll tell you later."

Meghan carried on with her reason for calling. "Well, I'm calling because I want us to go out. We have not had a chance to celebrate our new jobs and you only work twenty-four, seven." She ended with a pout.

Cali asked, "Where do you want to go, to the movies? That new Matt Damon movie is coming out this weekend."

Meghan said, "Oh no way honey, I mean, let's get dressed up and go out."

Cali moaned, "Meghan, you know I don't go out."

Megan's rebuttal seemed to hit a brick wall. "Girl, it's high time you started. We're two beautiful college educated and successful women and we need to meet some guys. There's this new club downtown we ought to check out. I hear it's where all of the hot entrepreneurs, entertainers, ball players, young doctors, and lawyers hang out."

Cali tried to talk her way out of it again, "Come on Meghan you know how I feel about that. You're gonna end up the only one of us getting asked to dance and the free drinks so I'm not even gonna waste my time. Besides, you know how I feel about dressing up anyway."

Meghan rallied on as if Cali hadn't mumbled a word. "Cali; just let us go out and have some good old fashioned fun like we used to. You don't have to wear a dress, just throw on some nice jeans and a shirt and let's do this! Even if you meet a friend you don't have to sleep with him, we just need to get out and unwind. I know I do and I want you there.

Cali was just as stubborn as Meghan was determined; "I don't have anything nice to wear which means I'll have to go shopping. And you know I can't walk in heels."

Meghan cackled as she shut down Cali's entire argument with her last statement, "Now Cali, what's my job? I dress people for a living or have you forgotten? I have you covered in all of the above."

Cali couldn't help but laugh along with her dear friend as she realized she wasn't going to win the debate. "Okay, okay, you're right, but where are we going? I don't want to be around a lot of smelly people and their smoking."

Megan campaigned, "No, from what I've heard this is a very nice club. Upscale even; it's called The Topple.

Intrigued by just the name Cali asked, "The Topple? Now what kind of club is that?"

Meghan coyly answered, "They call it The Topple because only people who are at the top of their industry go there. I mean people making well over six figures!"

"Humph, you know I'm not into people for their money." Cali retorted.

Meghan confirmed, "Well I am. Just go with me and let me find someone then I can take care of you when you're old and broke."

They laughed at their ongoing joke they've shared since high school. Cali wanted to know, "What time are you coming over?"

Meghan cooed into the phone, "I'll be over at your place about six o'clock."

Still unsure of whether she wanted to truly go or not, Cali muttered, "Okay and don't forget to bring me something to wear."

When Meghan arrived and rung Cali's doorbell she looked like she was frozen in time; she had no makeup on, her hair was still in her everyday work ponytail.

Cali tried talking her way out of going again, "Meg, I just don't know about this."

Meghan asked with a bit of impatience, "Cali do you trust me?"

She answered meekly, "Yes, you know I do."

Pinching her playfully on her cheeks, she ordered, "Then get up and get yourself in gear. Here check out this hot little number I found." Meghan handed Cali a very sexy black dress, but classy. And don't worry, I found a sexy pair of wedges to go with it."

Meghan gave further instructions of how she did not want Cali looking at herself until she was finished getting dressed. Meghan took Cali's soft shoulder length black hair and put it up in a soft French roll. She enhanced her face with just a little eye shadow and mascara. Cali's skin was so milky smooth she didn't need much makeup. And the three inch wedged heel eased Cali's mind and felt comfortable enough to run in. After all, she didn't need much height. She smiled at her dearest friend for always remembering her likes and dislikes when it came to really dressing up.

When Meghan took Cali to the mirror she was shocked to see how nice she looked as a woman. The beauty she saw staring back at her was overwhelming; she began to cry. She couldn't help but think, "If my daddy could see me now."

Meghan said, "Oh no you don't go messing up my master piece."

This made Cali laugh. She gingerly wiped her tears as she said, "You are completely crazy." Megan kept her promise she gave her a look she felt comfortable with.

When they arrived, it took a few minutes for the valet to hand them a ticket and park the car. The entrance wrapped around the building and everyone they past was beyond well dressed, from Chanel to Gucci to Roberto Cavalli; the men and women looked like they were ready for someone's runway. Cali had never seen so many BMW's, limos, and Mercedes in one place other than a car dealership. The club's atmosphere was electrifying everything was absolutely stunning.

Cali was beginning to feel a bit nervous and wanted to sit at the first table she saw, but Meghan wanted to sit at the bar. Stating her usual theory, she spoke above the music, "The guys need to know we're single, so the bar is the best spot to be seen."

But I'm not looking so can't we just find a nice table this time around please? Cali protested.

Meghan found two empty stools and pulled Cali towards the empty one and re-stated, "Like I said earlier, I am, so sit here with me."

Cali couldn't help but laugh, "You're serious aren't you?"

With her eyes bulging in delight Meghan replied, "Yep, as serious as that guy's tight booty."

Cali covered her face embarrassed at what her friend just said but she still found herself peeping between her fingers to see the tight booty; and it was tight.

The bartender came over to ask them what they wanted to drink.

Meghan requested in her flirtatious voice, "I'll have an apple martini."

Looking at Cali, he patiently waited. She was not a drinker and did not know what to order so she opted for something she usually drinks anyway, "Can you give me some lemon water?"

The handsome bartender smiled at the young ladies and said to them both, "Yes, an apple martini and lemon water coming right up." Meghan hurriedly reached towards the bartender. He paused. "Give her what I'm having please."

He looked over towards Cali for her approval. Giving in, she nodded yes. He chirped, "Okay two apple martinis coming right up." And then dapped away to fix their drink.

Meghan turned back to Cali, "We're going to have a good time even if it kills you."

They leaned into each other from a fit of laughter; the way they normally did at Meghan's antics. One of the things Cali always loved about Meghan is how she could always make her laugh; even when she didn't want to. In the midst of their bonding a well-dressed man appeared next to Meghan and asked her to dance. She looked at Cali to see if she would be fine; Cali gave her a nonchalant wave to go dance as she began to sip on the apple martini the bartender had just set in front of them. Watching her from the sidelines Cali smiled as she couldn't recall Meghan dancing so well in high school or college. Years had given her a bit of rhythm. When she finished dancing with the first gentlemen she came back to the bar to be with Cali and tasted her drink. Before she could take a second sip someone else was asking her to dance.

Before she left the bar she pointed her finger at the bartender and said giddily, "Look out for my friend."

That's one of the things Meghan did from the moment she and Cali became friends; she knew she was tough enough to take care of herself physically, but she helped protect Cali's heart. No one knew all Cali went through but Meghan from high school to college; staying up with her friend when she wanted to kill herself. Cali had a lot of pride and would never let anyone see her weakness until she met Meghan but going through the psychology program had helped her to except herself for who she was.

Chapter 5

Cali found herself smiling happily and bobbing her head to the music as she looked out towards the dance floor. There was a time she would've found herself a bit jealous and ready to go home but this time around she sat and watched her friend dance as she freely enjoyed herself. Thinking back, Cali knew she'd stolen a lot of Meghan's years of having fun and dating with her bouts of depression and low self-esteem; she'd given up quite a few dates whenever Cali called her in distress. So, Cali genuinely wanted her friend to have as much fun as she wanted and hoped she found the man of her dreams.

Just as Cali settled into the bar stool to finish her drink, she heard someone whisper over her shoulders, "Do you come here often?"

Cali turned around to see who was talking to her. To her surprise it was the handsome doctor that worked at West Wood Hospital; she'd seen him every morning ordering the same thing in the cafeteria; a muffin and a cup of tea.

Recognizing her too, he asked, "Haven't I seen you around West Wood?"

Cali shyly smiled, "Why, yes, I work in the psychology department."

"I've seen you around a couple of times in the cafeteria." He smiled along with her.

Cali was a little shocked that he'd noticed her too. She asked to keep the conversation going, not that she didn't already know he was a doctor; but she wanted to hear his French accent again. "What is it you do there?"

He answered proudly, "Well, I'm a doctor in internal medicine."

Nodding her head approvingly, Cali said with surprise, "Oh! Okay."

He reached for her hand to formally introduce himself, "I'm so sorry, I should've already said this but my name is Lance Roberts."

Taking his hand in hers, Cali tried to reply the way Meghan would reply, "Nice to meet you Dr. Roberts."

He chuckled, "Call me Lance. And what's your name?"

"Cali Evans" she answered.

He returned the nicety, "Nice to meet you Dr. Evans."

She smiled again and said "You can call me Cali."

Lance asked if she wanted something to drink. Cali held her half empty glass as if toasting, "We just ordered, but thank you anyway."

Meghan began sauntering her way back from the dance floor grinning from ear to ear. She'd spotted this handsome stranger talking to Cali before the song even ended and couldn't wait to be nosy.

Lance said, "I'll let you get back with your company. You ladies enjoy your night out." Staring fondly at Cali he continued. "I'll be seeing you around."

Cali couldn't help but to smile, "Okay." She answered.

Meghan came back fanning herself as if to be out of breath, dabbing a napkin around her neck and cleavage. She asked excitedly, "Who was that?"

Cali smiled before answering, "He works at Westwood."

Nudging her playfully in the ribs, Meghan begged, "Sooo, spill it girl. What does he do?"

Cali responded casually; not wanting to sound as excited as she felt, "He's a doctor."

At that moment the waiter set their second round of drinks down and Meghan picked up her glass to toast. Cali picked up her drink too.

Meghan smiled devilishly and winked before saying, "Here's to real-estate."

*****

The next morning at work Cali got a phone call from her mother; concerned she had not heard from her and was wondering how she'd been doing. Cali had not been keeping in touch with her mother as much as she knew she should. To hurry her off of the phone, she said she would be over to see her as soon as she lightened her case load at work.

But, before Cali could hang up, her mother asked her the dreaded question she'd grown to hate hearing with grave concern in her voice; if she'd been keeping her appointments with Dr. P.

Cali answered in frustration; "For what mom? I've been feeling fine."

Her mother paused and said, "Oh okay, but come and see me. I've missed you."

Cali stepped all around her mother's emotion filled statement and asked. "Have you seen or heard from dad?"

Her mother replied. "Yes, he calls from time to time."

"Mom, how can you put up with that?" Cali started with her usual tirade when it came to him, their marriage, and his unexplained absence. "He didn't come out and say he was leaving, but mom he still has abandoned you. He hasn't lived in that home since I was about five or six years old. Mom, you could have been set free to move on with your life and find love with someone else instead of waiting for him to come around." Not realizing or caring for the moment about her mother's silent tears she continued. "Mom please tell me the truth . . . did dad leave you because of me? If he did then tell him I don't live there anymore. He can come home now."

Cali found herself getting upset and decided to cut herself off before she said something she'd really regret. Even after learning about human behavior and earning her degree in psychology, she couldn't understand why he hated her so much. Before she was born her parents loved each other; she saw pictures of them together looking very happy.

Not wanting to upset her any further; Cali muttered, "Mom I have to hang up. I have a client."

"Okay honey. Please come and see me when you can. I miss seeing you." her mother pleaded with hope.

Cali answered, "Sure mom, I'll talk to you later."

When Cali hung up she sat at her desk with her head in her hands; she began rubbing her forehead as if to rub her thoughts away. Interrupting her moment of peace and quiet, there was a knock on the door.

"Come in." she answered with a perkiness she didn't feel. She was surprised, but very happy to see the Lance.

He said, "So this is where you hide out. I thought I would see you in the cafeteria today."

She smiled and responded, "I didn't get a chance to eat. I have a case load of files to look through."

Lance stood there with his hands casually behind his back. He reciprocated her smile and brought them forward; he held up two bags and said, "Then my thoughts were right. I brought you some lunch and wondered maybe I could join you."

Cali's stomach rumbled at realizing how hungry she was. "Oh you did? Well what's on the menu?"

Lance explained, "I didn't know what you liked, so I got turkey, tuna, salad, and soup."

Cali licked her lips and replied, "That works for me. I guess I can stop for a minute."

She cleaned her desk off to make room for their lunch. He spread out their small buffet. They sampled everything and ended up talking for hours. Lance made Cali forget that just hours ago she was upset after talking with her mother. She gushed to Lance how lunch was just what the doctor ordered. They laughed easily together.

Cali offered, "We must do this again sometimes."

He asked, "Hmm, what about tomorrow? Have dinner with me."

He scared her; she felt things were already moving a little too fast so her first response was, "I can't."

Lance looked away embarrassed, "I'm sorry. I guess I am moving too fast? I thought after talking with me theses past months you felt comfortable enough to go to dinner, once again I apologies."

Cali didn't want him to feel that way because there was something about Lance she trusted in spite of just getting to know him; like Meghan. She explained, "Oh no; I have a late appointment with a patient and I still have to respond to some of these reports, but what about Friday? My calendar is free after three o' clock."

He released the breath he didn't realized he'd been holding and answered, "That sounds good. Would six be okay? I promise I'll have you home before you turn into a pumpkin."

She laughed and shook her head, "Sure, that will be fine."

Lance stood up to walk out of the door when Cali thought to ask, "Wait, where would you like for me to meet you?"

He chided, "A lady should always be picked up and besides I want to surprise you."

After lance left Cali could not wait to call Meghan. When she answered the phone Cali blurted into the phone without even saying hello; "Guess who's going out to dinner and with whom?"

Megan guessed, "Hmmm, let me see." Giggled knowingly and continued. "The dear doctor asked you out to dinner!"

Cali said "Yes! And I tell you Meghan if it wasn't for Lance I would have pulled my hair out."

Meghan probed. "Why? What happened?"

Going into her usual complaint, "You know I get upset after talking to my mother. Well, first she asked me if I was still keeping my appointments with Dr. P. I told her no, I'm feeling fine and of course that upsets her. Then, I asked her had she heard from dad. She said, from time to time. I said mom why are you still waiting for him when he has abandoned your marriage? He's never given you a reason for leaving and for all we know he could have another family out there. I know he still sends her financial support; he pays all the bills, but Meghan I feel like it is something they have not told me. I don't know what it is but there is something."

Meghan stated, "Cali it could be something that happened between them that they don't want you to know about."

Cali lamented in frustration, "I would rather know so I can make some sense out of all of this." Cali took a deep breath and continued, "You know what? I'm going to leave this alone for today. I had a wonderful lunch brought to me by the handsome doctor. And that's when he asked me to dinner I told him no at first because I thought things were moving too fast, but Meghan there's something that I like and trust about him, just how I felt about you when we first met. It feels . . . right."

Meghan cooed back with love for her long-time friend, "That is so sweet; you're going on your first date.

Cali begged, "Please don't call it a date, I am just having dinner with a colleague who is now a new friend."

Cali mentioned to her before she moved onto a different subject, "Don't forget, it's Friday at six p.m. So you know I need you there early to help get me ready."

"Well, if he's going to be just a friend, just throw on some jeans." Meghan continued with her one woman show.

Cali said, "Ha. Ha. Very funny Meg; just be at my place please to help me dress.

Meghan laughed and finally said, "Okay, okay, you know I have your back." She immediately thought to ask, "Cali; is he married?"

Cali paused and slightly frowned, "I didn't ask, but I didn't see a ring or a ring mark on his finger but I will definitely find out."

Meghan clapped happily and announced loudly into the phone. "Well so far so good."

Chapter 6

Before they could finish their latest date dishing, Cali's second line rang with an incoming call. She told Meghan she would talk to her later. The call was from Jena Sargent; a referral patient who turned out to be a good candidate for the adoption program being she had been consulting since the beginning of her pregnancy and had not changed her mind about giving her baby up for adoption. She given birth to her baby just the day before so Cali's first thought was she was calling because she had changed her mind about the adoption, but it was the other way around. Cali told Jena she'd be right up to talk with her.

When she arrived Jena was sobbing. Cali walked quickly to her bedside and placed a hand on her shoulder before asking her what happened.

Jena exclaimed with worry, "When the baby was circumcised they burned part of his penis. The doctor's told the adoptive parents they wanted to change him to a girl. They said that they did not want to deal with something like that and could not adopt him. They left!"

Hearing this made Cali's head spin. "What do you mean by change him to a girl?"

Jena answered. "That's what the adoptive parents told me. The doctor has not been in here to talk to me."

The air gushed out of Cali's chest as she tried to calm Jena down and stated. "Let me talk with your nurse so I can find out what the hell they are talking about and excuse my French, but this is crazy." Telling Jena she'd be right back, Cali went to the nurse's station and asked for the Jena's nurse.

An elderly lady with tortoise shell eyeglasses and a tight high bun answered like a drill sergeant. "I am. May I help you?"

Cali introduced herself and asked the nurse about the baby and if what the patient had heard was true. She was highly concerned no one had come to talk to Jena about it even though she was giving the baby up for adoption and she wanted to give her the correct information, in case there was some kind of misunderstanding. The nurse spoke confidently, "The adoptive parents were told because they were going to be the legal guardians."

Cali pressed on with her questions, "What is this about changing the baby to a girl?"

The nurse could sense the tension in her voice before answering, "Well, the penis was burned during the circumcision procedure. Because of that the baby won't be able to function and they suggested changing him to a girl. Actually that would be best at this young age."

Completely astonished at how casual she sounded, Cali probed, "Have they ever done this before?"

Staring over her eye glasses, she took a deep breath to calm her own nerves from all of the questioning. "I only know of one since I have been here. It was about twenty-six years ago."

Cali wondered about this child. "Would you happen to know how is she doing?"

The nurse thought hard before she responded. "Hmm, I don't know. I heard the family broke up and we couldn't keep up with the child."

"Have there been any other cases other than this hospital?" Cali was heated now; she couldn't believe her ears.

The nurse continued, "Oh yes, it's being done more than people know. Some come out good and some have a tough time. The main problem is they usually cannot identify with who they are."

Gasping in disbelief and disgust, Cali said, "That's horrible! Does the news know anything about this?"

Removing her glasses to inspect and clean them, the nurse let out a small sigh, "Most families are too embarrassed to talk about it and don't want to bring attention to their child."

Cali massaged her temples as she propped her elbows on the counter and asked, "So they just let these children just wander around trying to figure this out on their own? Do they at least tell them they were changed?"

She placed her glasses back onto her face and gave Cali a tired look. "I don't think so."

Cali kept going with her line of questioning, surprised at how open and candid this nurse was with this information; as if she was simply speaking about the weather. "Don't these doctor's know or have they even considered that just because they change their body you have not changed their minds?" Cali wondered aloud. "Good grief! When will man accept God does not make mistakes?!?" She stopped herself from saying anything further. Her side of the conversation was drawing unwanted attention. Cali closed her eyes quickly blinking and ended their conversation; "Thank you for being so honest with me."

Her mind was racing a mile a minute but she felt better in being able to give her patient all the information she needed to make a good decision. As Cali walked away the nurse had no clue she was just talking to the child she saw changed to a girl twenty-six years ago. When Cali returned to Jena's room she was alert, not crying; but just very excited and full of optimism; a totally different mood from before.

She smiled and quietly spoke, "Ms. Cali, I am not giving my baby up for adoption. I am going to keep my baby and I'm not going to change him to a girl. God made him a boy and that is what he is going to be. Whatever he needs in life I believe God will provide it for him. I have seen some people born with no arms and God showed them how to use their feet or their mouth and God put people in their lives to love them. And this was a wake-up call for me. I'm always trying to find the easy way out, but not this time. I am going to start taking care of my responsibility."

Cali smiled but said, "I think you should talk with a lawyer. I cannot discuss anything about that to you, but they can. Are you sure that you want to keep your baby?"

Nodding firmly, she answered, "Yes, I'm sure."

Cali reached for her hand to offer reassurance and said, "Well, I will note your files of your decision and recommend a case manager to help you once you and your baby leave the hospital. If you have any more questions call me, okay? And good luck Jena with your son."

*****

On the way home Cali started thinking about what the nurse had said about the baby that was changed twenty-six years ago. Cali thought to herself, "I was born there twenty-six years ago. My parents split and I did feel like I was a boy. But I think I have gotten better and I'm excited about dating a handsome man. Could that baby she was talking about be me? Why didn't she remember me or have I changed that much? Could this be the secret my parents have been hiding all of these years? Oh God. . . is that child me?"

Her cell phone rang; interrupting the rush of thoughts raging through her mind like a tornado. She was sitting at a red light, glanced down, and smiled at recognizing Lance's number on the caller ID. It seemed as if he always rescued her from emotional turmoil.

She answered, "You know I am going to change your name to knight in shining armor."

Laughing, Lance asked, "Why?"

"Because you always show up or call just when I need to be brought in from a whirl wind situation."

He smiled as he spoke, "I'm glad to be there for you Cali. I was working late and couldn't get you off of my mind. I enjoyed lunch and most of all I enjoyed your conversation."

Cali politely interjected before she forgot to ask, "There is something I need to ask you."

Lance perceived her question and beat her to it by saying, "The answer is no."

"How presumption of you," she said with laughter, "but you don't even know what I wanted to ask you."

He said, "Any smart lady, of which, I think you are will find out if a man is married before getting involved in any way."

He could hear her sigh of relief through the speaker. "Well I'm glad we got that out of the way." Cali continued, "I can't believe that all of those attractive lady doctors and nurses at the hospital have not tried to tie you down."

Lance admitted, "I did date one lady there for a couple of months, but she wanted to date a doctor not me. That is why I find you so interesting. You make me feel like a normal relationship is possible."

After a moment of silence, Lance spoke up. "Hello? Cali? Did I lose you?"

Cali answered apologetically, "Oh Lance, I'm sorry. My mind just rambled. I had an unusual case today that has my nerves in a bundle."

"Is it any thing you can talk about?" he asked with trepidation.

"Lance, I have a patient whose baby had an unfortunate accident at the hospital. They burned the baby's penis during circumcision and now they want to change the baby boy to a girl. Have you ever heard of anything like that before?"

He wasn't surprised as he answered, "Yes."

"Well, how do you feel about that?" she wanted to know.

He shrugged as if she could see him through the phone, "I never gave it much thought but if you think about it; it may have given some child a chance for a normal life."

Unconvinced, she still replied, "I never thought of it that way."

This conversation felt like it was definitely headed in a direction to being awkward. He began wrapping up the call. "Well I have a few more rounds to make. I'll see you tomorrow at six. Get some sleep; leave your work in your brief case."

Sure she could leave the case in her briefcase, but what he didn't know was it was definitely in her mind; and that's what worried her the most.

Chapter 7

The next morning Cali woke up bright and early and went to medical records. Something in her heart made her want to find out if perhaps she was the baby they changed twenty-six years ago. She found her files and her birth certificate. The moments that tormented her since hearing about Jena's baby caused her palms to sweat and stick to the folders she pulled from their slot. She nervously opened it and peeked inside. To her dismay nothing was abnormal in her files. She felt so relieved she went to her office and called Meghan to remind her of her date tonight.

When Meghan answered Cali inquired, "Meg you didn't forget that I'm going on my date tonight, did you?"

Meghan replied, "No, I didn't forget. But I will not be there. I have a hot date too. I'm going out with Doug."

"Wow, okay then." Cali went into nosey best friend mode. "Who is that?"

Meghan tried to jar her memory. "You know that cute bartender at The Topple who served us drinks until we had to call a cab?"

Recalling the horrible hang over she had, Cali groaned, "Yeah, don't remind me. But I do remember him; he was a nice guy, but I thought you were looking for real estate?"

Meghan revealed to Cali, "He owns that place girlfriend! He just likes to hide as the bartender so the women won't hit on him and that gives him a chance to weed them out. Isn't that genius?"

Cali smiled along with her friend, "Yeah, but how did you two start talking?

"I slipped him a note and told him thanks for looking out for you. He was like it was going to cost you. That's when he asked me for my number and I gave it to him. I thought he was cute the moment I saw him. Well, he called me a couple of days later and we talked for a long time. That's when he told me that he owned The Topple and was ready to settle down with the right person."

"Meghan that's great! But how am I going to put an outfit together tonight?"

Meghan clucked, "Oh silly you know I got your back, do you think I will let you go out on your first date looking like a train wreck?"

They both laughed. Megan continued, "I left everything on your bed. Just wear your hair up the way I showed you with that dress. You already do a good job with your make up, lip gloss, and a little mascara. You don't need much; the rest of the night is up to you."

When Cali got home she felt a major sense of relief as she saw the beautiful dress and the nice shoes that Meghan had left out for her. Cali's shape was a little boxy, but for a man she had nice legs. The dress did not cling but it still was very sexy. Cali took a shower and got a glass of wine to take the edge off of her nerves. As she started to get dressed she began to have second thoughts. All kinds of doubtful thoughts dribbled through her mind like rain drops. She thought, "This is going too fast. What are we going to talk about? I can't dance. Oh heck, I've never been on a date. I just cannot do this."

The doorbell rang. Cali paused as if she wasn't going to answer. The doorbell rang again.

Cali called out, "Just a minute." as she gave herself a last look in the mirror. "Who is it?"

He said, "It's Doctor Roberts." In just that second she felt at ease because he made the date seem a little formal and not so personal. When she opened the door he had a big smile on his face.

Cali wanted to know, "What is the big grin for?"

He nodded toward her dress with appreciation. "Blue is my favorite color." He glanced down at the navy blue suit he was wearing. "Are you ready?"

"Why yes I am Doctor Roberts." Cali smiled into his face. "Where are we going?"

"I can't, it's a surprise." He stated as Cali grabbed her shawl and headed for the door.

Lance opened the door and let Cali walk out ahead of him. He held his hand out for the key to lock the door and handed it back to her after locking it. Cali thought to herself; "Is this how a woman should be treated; because this man is doing everything right."

Lance went even further in being a gentleman and opened the door for Cali to get in his custom Mercedes. She watched him through the rear view mirrors as he walked around to the driver's side, as he got in Cali complimented; "Nice car."

Lance smiled as he answered, "As a kid I always wanted one so when I became a doctor I rewarded myself. Do you think that was too vain of me?"

"No, after all of the hours spent studying and working those long hours as an intern, I think you truly deserved it. And the mere fact that you're even asking my opinion tells me it was not vanity; you honestly wanted this car and it is absolutely beautiful. So now are you going to tell me where we're going?"

He reached above their heads and opened his sun roof. The weather was balmy with few clouds in the sky and the stars twinkled as if they held a secret of their own. The breeze rustled layers of his hair. He turned to her with his gorgeous smile and said calmly, "The weather is beautiful; the stars are out; just sit back and enjoy the ride. And enjoy the ride she did.

They rode for what seemed like an hour as Cali sat up from her reclined position in the passenger seat; taking notice they were no longer in the city. The countryside roamed past with ranch style houses lit up from the inside. Horses and cows grazed in the twilight. She pondered aloud, "Lance, what are we doing out here in country?"

Lance chuckled aloud not offering a reply.

Cali continued to marvel; she hadn't been out in the area for a few years and it was still so beautiful and serene to her. "Ah! And there's the lake; Meghan and I used to come and hang out here during our summer breaks in college!"

As they drove up she saw a restaurant was now on the lake. She could see the outline of the building etched with tiny star lights. They drove over a beautiful draw bridge that took them to the restaurant parking lot; Cali marveled at how it kind of reminded her of the bridge from the movie, The Bridges Over Madison County, except it had ivy growing along the railings with more star lights twinkling between the vines; it definitely gave off the vibe for romance. She recalled seeing this island that sat in the very center of the lake from summers past. She laughed and shook her head as she remembered how people would take a boat out to the island to do things other than just sunbathe. There were only a few other cars in the parking lot. From the looks of it, Cali guessed it was either a place not many knew about yet or it was just so exclusive that there was never a huge crowd. As they entered the restaurant Cali was amazed at the décor. It had a three hundred sixty degree view; you could see the lake where ever you were seated. The dark hardwood floors and see through fire place gave it a rustic, but cozy feel. Each table was draped with champagne colored linen cloths and a vase filled with baby breath; the booths were half circles with sheer drapes that added a touch of intimacy.

The hostess asked them where they wanted to sit; a table or a booth; they chose the booth. When they sat down Cali immediately took off her shoes, she was not use to wearing heels and her feet felt like swollen sausages in just the little time she'd had them on. When Lance asked her what would she like to drink; he was surprised when she answered champagne.

He said to the waiter, "Champagne it is. Please bring us a bottle of your best." He looked back towards Cali, "The lobster dinner is really good here."

Cali smiled and answered, "I would like to try it then."

Lance ordered two lobster dinners. They enjoyed their excellent gourmet meal with easy flowing conversation and open laughter.

Cali asked, "It's been years since I've been out this way myself, but how did you find this place? This area has always been a wonderful little spot for a get away without getting away."

He replied, "One day I was in a head clearing mood and just took a ride out here to the country and found this place." She nodded in understanding about having those types of moments. The champagne was setting in on both of them and Lance asked her to dance.

Cali stammered, "I . . . I don't know how."

Lance stood up and took her by the hand and suavely said, "Don't worry, I'll show you." He led her to the dance floor, took her into his arms and gingerly pulled her into his embrace. She laid her head on his shoulders and followed his lead. The pianist played what sounded like some Frank Sinatra covers. She enjoyed being in his space for four songs straight. When they got back to their table they ordered some coffee before the long ride home.

When they arrived back at her home he was as gentlemanly as he was when they'd left. He asked for her keys and opened the door for her to let her in. He stood in threshold as she laid her keys and bag on the table. She turned back to face him, "I had a wonderful evening."

He gazed before answering, "It was the best time I've had in a long time."

They looked into each other's eyes before Lance took Cali's face in his hands and kissed her forehead lovingly. Lance knew that there was something special about Cali and that he would have to handle her with kitten gloves. Cali closed her eyes at his kiss and was very happy that he kissed her forehead, but a little sad that he did not kiss her lips; because of the wonderful evening, she was ready. When he left, she closed the door and rested her back against it letting out a sigh of relief. Her life was finally making sense.

When Lance got back into his car he muttered aloud; "I think I found the woman I'm going to marry."

*****

That Saturday morning; Cali got a chance to sleep in late and she totally enjoyed reminiscing on her date with Lance. She had never felt so relaxed and carefree around a man before. She wondered where all of these feelings were coming from being she'd never felt this way about a guy before. The doorbell rang rudely interrupting her thoughts. She wondered it could be as she peeped through the peep hole; she smiled widely seeing it was Meghan. She rushed to open the door with a flourish. She was so happy to see her with the both of them being so busy lately. They'd talked on the phone, but it wasn't the same as seeing her friend face to face. Cali didn't have a sibling so Meghan was the next best thing. When Cali opened the door she quickly hugged her friend and grabbed her by the hand to pull her inside.

She asked immediately, "What all have you been up to since you've been going on trips and flying everywhere with Doug."

Meghan noticed Cali's glow, "Me? What's up with you? What have you been up to?"

Cali stopped and thought quickly, "Oh, no, no, no; not what you're thinking. Lance and I simply enjoyed each other's company. The dress you left for me to wear happened to be his favorite color. He took me to a restaurant in the country. You remember Lake Mulligan; they've built a restaurant on that island that sits it the center of it. Meghan, it was so nice. I even danced. And you know how I feel about dancing and I did in my heels at that.

Meghan bowled over in laughter on the sofa, "You're kidding!"

Cali gushed, "Meg, he's doing everything right. He was perfect gentlemen last night. And when he dropped me off, he held my face in his hands and kissed me on my forehead. I had such a wonderful time I started to plant a big one on his lips, but the whole night was just right and I wanted to keep it that way."

Meghan teased, "Cali, it has been about five months give the man a kiss already."

Meghan continued joking about how much of a gentleman he was, "Cali you have been talking to him for five months now! Wow, time moves fast when you're having clean fun but goodness, that man sure does have restraint."

Cali bragged, "I guess I'm worth the wait."

Meghan agreed, "Girl, you must be."

Cali blushed, "I know and when I do everything will be right. Besides I think he finds me to be a challenge. He likes me because he knows I am not trying to be with him because he's a doctor. Plus, you know I have never dated. This is all new for me. I'm not like you, I never had feelings for man, but I like him because he is genuinely nice to me and very patient. I've grown to trust him with my heart like I did with you Meghan." Feeling herself getting emotional she hurriedly changed the subject. "Anyway Meghan, enough about me; you look different. Did you change your hair? You just look different in a nice, glowy, kind of way."

Meghan smiled conspiratorially and allowed a pause to hang as heavy as fog before squealing, "No I didn't change my hair, but you're going to be an aunt and a maid of honor all at one time! Can you handle that?" she asked as she wiggled her ring finger with an enormous diamond that Doug had given her.

Cali hollered with excitement, "Meg, are you kidding me?"

She went on to explain as she repositioned herself on the sofa, "That is where we were yesterday; finding out if I was pregnant or not. When the doctor said that I was, we went out to celebrate and Doug asked me to marry him, and I said yes! I didn't know he had already bought a ring. He told me he was going to propose on Christmas, but it was no better time than now."

Meghan stood up and grabbed Cali's hand, pulling her over to the window and told her to look out into the parking lot. She pointed to silver BMW and said, "He also bought me that. He didn't want me driving my old bat mobile anymore. I don't know why he said that I still like my bat mobile. Didn't she get us around in college?"

They laughed and chimed in unison, "She sure did!"

With all kinds ideas for a baby and wedding shower already swimming around in her head, Cali asked, "When is the baby due and when are you getting married?"

Rubbing her non-existent belly already, Meghan said, "I'm only six weeks. And we're getting married in two months, that way I won't look like a balloon in my wedding dress."

The two best friends enjoyed a few more hours of catching up with each other's lives and making plans for Meghan's wedding shower over their favorite foods and the natural camaraderie they've shared since high school. Cali was truly happy for her dear friend but desperately hoped her marriage wouldn't change their friendship.

*****

After Meghan left even though it was a little late, Cali decided to visit her mother as she had promised. She wanted to tell her about Lance and tell her the good news about Meghan, but when she pulled up to her mother's house her father's car was in the driveway. When Cali saw his car, dread filled her chest like heavy bricks; she drove on by. She was not in the mood to deal with her father. No matter what she did he showed no interest in her or her life. He didn't even show up to her graduations. His last words she remembers him speaking to her were to act like a girl and she had been for over ten years, but it still has not made their relationship any better. But Cali was still glad that he was still keeping in touch with her mom. She hoped this meant he was living back home, so her mother would not be alone.

Chapter 8

The next morning Cali called her mother to tell her she came by but she had seen her father's car in the driveway and she did not want to disturb them. She asked her mom was he home to stay.

She sadly mentioned, "No he came by to pick up some things."

Cali became instantly frustrated; she didn't understand why she continually allowed it to anger her after all of this time. "Mom, what is wrong with him? Is he living with someone else?"

She sniffed into the phone. "Cali, don't start. I don't know; I didn't ask him. Please understand once and for all, there were things that happened between us that you just don't understand."

Cali was determined and wasn't giving up. She figured her mother must've forgotten how persistent she could be. "Well you should try explaining it to me because my childhood and young adult life was turned upside down. And you know what mom? I have been blaming dad, but you are just as much to blame because you know why dad left and why he feels the way he does about me. Through all of my turmoil you and dad have been very selfish; only caring about your feeling's and not mine. I will not be a part of this loveless house hold anymore." She took a deep breath; trying to keep her tears from falling. Her throat closed with emotion. It took a few seconds to speak again. "Mom I love you and have never wanted to disrespect you, but I will never come back into that house until you or dad decides to tell me what you have been hiding from me." She didn't give her mother any room to respond. "I came by to share some good news with you mom; I wanted to tell you about the guy I met and to tell you Meghan is getting married."

Cali's mother stuttered nervously, "You, you met a guy? Have you been keeping your appointments with Dr. P.?"

Cali held the phone away from her ear and stared at it in angry disbelief. "Why are you talking about him now, when I just told you about the good things that are happening for me and Meghan? Dr. P has nothing at all to do with this! How did he even fit into this conversation? I don't believe you, goodbye mother." When Cali hung up she had never been so angry with her mom. Usually it was towards her father, but this time Cali was angrier than she'd ever been as she yelled at the phone as if it was her mother, "Why was she still bugging me about going to this doctor?!? It is really beyond getting on my nerves." Cali reached for the telephone to call Meghan but remembered she was pregnant and didn't want to stress her out with her issues. Cali took a deep breath and tried to encourage herself. "I'm going to get through this." She wrung her hands and wrapped her arms around herself to shake the chill of anxiety that made its way down her spine. Just as she started to get up from the table her pager started to buzz; it was a page from the hospital. Cali glared at the number for the return call. She recognized it was from Jena, her patient that refused to have her baby's sex changed.

Cali was a little nervous of what would make her patient call her on the weekend. She took deep breath as she dialed the call back number. "Hi Jena, this is Dr. Evans how can I help you?"

Jena cried into the phone, "Dr. Evans I told the doctor that I didn't want my baby's sex changed and he said he was going to call children services."

Running her hands over her signature ponytail, Cali asked, "Call them for what?"

Jena was in a full out breakdown, "I don't know. I don't understand Dr. Evans. What do I do?" as she continued to cry.

Cali tried her best to sound reassuring. "Calm down. Everything's going to be okay. It's the weekend, their offices are closed. I'll be there to see you first thing Monday morning, okay?"

Jena sniffled into the phone, "Yes, Dr. Evans please come by; I don't want them to do anything to my son.   And now that I've decided to keep him; I don't want to lose him."

After attempting to reassure Jena again Cali was finally able to calm her enough to hang up and get some rest. She was highly concerned for Jena. She'd had the baby by caesarean so she was under the impression that was the reason why she had not been able to leave the hospital. Cali found herself worrying all night about her patient. Little sleep and bad dreams made for one terrible night. By four-thirty the following morning, Cali gave up and fixed herself a cup of chamomile tea.

That Sunday morning found Cali sipping her second cup of tea, staring out into the city as it got its start for the day, and hoping the tea would calm her enough to get a few more hours of sleep. But it never came; she received a call from Lance who wanted to let her know how nice of a time he had on their dinner date. He asked if she wanted to meet him for lunch at work the next day. She answered tiredly, "I'll have to check my schedule; plus see a patient regarding an urgent issue, but if I can it would be in the cafeteria.

Lance let her know, "Oh that's fine. Just call me when you're free." Sensing her mood he told her he'd let her go and to have a good night's rest.

"I'll try." Cali stretched and rotated her neck as she pressed the end button on her phone. She hadn't meant to sound so blah towards him; she made a mental note to tell him some more about her family life if she got the chance. That night when she went to sleep she was tortured with another dream; this one more disturbing than the night before. She was in the hospital walking down the hall when she heard a boy yelling for help. When she looked around to see why no one was answering his call she noticed there was no one sitting at the nurse's station nor was there a nurse in sight. As the boy kept yelling his voice seem to get older; now it seems the voice is from a young man. Cali yelled out, "Where are you?" The voice was coming from one of the hospital rooms. As Cali opened the door she heard the yell for help getting louder. Feeling relieved at finding him, Cali entered the room. She noticed a pool of blood on the floor; realizing this young man must be badly hurt. Cali yelled again, "Where are you?" She didn't see anyone in the bed. Her eyes scanned the room frantically but her vision was blurred. She heard a noise on the other side of the bed; as she made her way around to the other side of the bed she saw a young man squatted on the floor facing the wall and wearing a hospital gown. Cali reached for him as she asked him, "Can I help you get back onto the bed?" The young man didn't answer; Cali touched his shoulders and asked him, "Are you okay? What's your name?" The young man slowly turned and stood up; his gown was drenched in blood from the waist down. He mumbled, "My name is Cali." With each step he said; "My name is Cali." He reached out for her; she began to back away from him causing her to fall into the IV that was hung on his bed. She screamed, "Stay away from me!" Scrambling to get her balance, she was able to get up and ran out of the room. As she ran and screamed for help, she saw Dr. P walking down the hall with two orderlies. Cali stopped him by frantically yanking on his arm. "Dr. P, help me! There is a boy that was yelling for help. When I went to help him he had blood all down his gown and he said his name was Cali; my name. I never told him my name! I think he's crazy!" Cali pulled Dr. P down the hallway, back to the room where she had found the young man. She pointed to the door. "Here, this is the room he's in." And when they opened the door, the room was empty and clean as if no one had ever been in the room. Cali looked around confused and said, "Maybe he's in the other room." When they went to the room next to it; it was clean as well. Cali turned to tell Dr. P, "I'm not crazy! Everything I said was true!" Noticing a nurse slowly approaching her with a syringe; ready to sedate her, she screamed, "Wait! What are you doing? It's not me! It's not me!"

The alarm clock blared loudly; jarring her out of her sleep. Her skin felt clammy; her heart raced and felt like she'd run a marathon. She looked over at the clock; it was five o' clock in the morning. Still trying to gather her thoughts, Cali sat straight up and looked around her room; blinking rapidly to make sure she was still in her own bed. That dream had felt so real. She had never had a dream so frightening. She could not figure out what would cause a dream like that. Sitting on the side of the bed, Cali tried to make sense of the dream and its meaning. Thinking so hard gave her a headache and no use in going back to sleep so she got up and took a shower; one of the longest she'd ever taken. She tried with all of her might to wash that dream out of her mind.

Settling back into bed, she turned on the television to try and distract her thoughts and to keep from reliving her dream. Glancing at the clock again with a sigh, it blinked six thirty a.m. in red as if in warning. Normally she would be leaving to go to the hospital around this time to look over her schedule and to eat breakfast in the cafeteria, but after that disturbing dream, she decided to eat at home. Thinking of how she worked on the lower floor of the hospital; early in the mornings were kind of creepy. As eight thirty crept upon her, she prepared to leave for work. The phone rang just as she was about to open the door and it startled her; her nerves were really shook. Cali answered the phone nervously.

Meghan swallowed hard; feeling her stomach lurch, this time not from morning sickness. "What's wrong Cali?"

She managed stooping to fix her shoe, "Oh hi Meghan. I was just on my way to work"

Meghan breathed into the phone, "I'm not going to keep you. I just felt the need to call and see how you're doing. You don't sound so good. Are you sure you're okay?"

Cali pauses and sat down heavily on the sofa. "No, it's okay. I'm not in a rush to get there after the dream I had last night."

"Poor thing; no wonder you sound so spooked. I'm glad I called." Meghan was already beginning to sound like a mother as she continued; "What kind of dream did you have that has you not wanting to go to work?"

The lost sleep was fast catching up to her as she yawned. Cali shook her head to give herself a jolt. "I will fill you in later. You're the one who called Meg; are you alright? Is the baby okay?"

Meghan chuckled lovingly, "Yeah we're fine. Like I said, something told me to call and check on you. Don't forget to tell me later about this dream. You sound kind of out of it. I can't put my finger on what I'm trying to say . . . just not yourself. Oh and I also wanted us to go looking for bridal gowns and a maid of honor dress this evening, will you be able to make it?"

Hearing mention of the wedding made Cali smile. "That will be great! I need some time out with my friend anyway. What time are we going to meet?"

Meghan fought hard to keep her excitement at bay when her friend sounded so down. She hoped their dress hunting will pull her out of whatever funk she's in. She asked, "Is five fine?"

"Sure, five is fine. I have to meet with a patient today and meeting Lance for lunch. I'm not sure if anything else has been added to my calendar but I should be out of there in time. If not, you know I'll call you so we can try and reschedule."

Meghan said, "Seems like things are getting serious. How are things with you two?"

Cali admitted, "Actually, it's a little bit too good to be true. I think I better pick up the pace with him though. I don't want him to get away." She laughed softly. "So far he's been initiating everything we do and I don't want him thinking I'm just interested in remaining friends, but look I'm running late and I promised my client I would see her this morning. Where are we meeting?"

Meghan gave a quick run-down, "It's a new place down town. I'll meet you at Ruby's Diner; it's down the street from there."

"Okay, I have to get to work. I'll see you then! Love ya!" Cali placed the phone onto the charger, grabbed her keys, and headed towards the door again.

On the drive to work Cali had this weird feeling come over her about her patient, she didn't know what it was but the thought of her voice and how she asked that she please come to see her; then that awful dream she had made her shutter, almost run a red light, and almost hit a pedestrian. After profusely apologizing to the frightened middle aged lady, she gathered herself enough to finish making the drive into work. As Cali approached the hospital she saw flashing lights near the front entrance.   An ambulance blocked the entrance to the parking area which brought more frustration. Cali didn't normally curse, but she muttered as she tried to maneuver her car around the commotion; "What the hell is going on?" She could not park in the hospital; the traffic guard directed her back towards the street; telling her she had to park down the street and walk back to the hospital for right now. When she finally reached the hospital she approached a security officer she hadn't seen around before, "What's going on? I work here and had trouble getting into the parking area just now."

The young man, who looked like he should still be in high school, shook his head sadly, "We had a jumper; someone jumped from the 7th floor."

"Thank you!" she quickly answered as her stomach instantly went into knots, she ran into the hospital and found the nearest elevator. It felt like an eternity to get to seventh floor. There were a lot of police officers outside of Jena's room.

She hurried over to the nurse's station to ask, "Where is Jena?" and that's when the nurse confirmed nonchalantly she had jumped. Cali wanted to give in to all of her whirling emotions as she thought of how she'd promised to come in to see her; bile rose to the back of her throat as she wondered if her visit would've made a difference. She stared into the room; the police was questioning her roommate at the moment.

Cali found the courage to ask the nurse who went about her business as if nothing detrimental had occurred; "Why would she have jumped? Jena just called me on Friday and I told her I would see her this morning." Her pacing made the nurse look up from the computer with a look of sympathy. "So why would she want to kill herself?"

The nurse leaned over the countertop, reached out for Cali's arm, beckoning her to come closer, and glanced around nervously before whispering, "Saturday she was upset because she found out they had went ahead and changed her baby to a girl."

Cali gasped with her hand on her chest. She thought her heart would beat right through her shirt and slide to the floor. "They did what! Why? She did not want her baby changed to a girl. She wanted to leave him as he was. Who gave the hospital the authorization to perform that surgery?"

The nurse blinked sorrowfully and shrugged, "I don't know I only work Monday through Thursday; I'm only going by what was written in the weekend nurses notes here."

Cali wondered aloud, "Is she still here?"

Shaking her head as she clicked her ink pen annoyingly, "No, she gave her statement and left."

"What time did this happen?" Cali wanted to know.

The nurse answered solemnly, "Mmm, I think about five a.m."

Chapter 9

Cali's thoughts went into overdrive; that was time she woke up from that horrible dream she had. She had a gut feeling that somehow all of this was connected. After the detectives left Cali made her way to Jena's room; she looked around and her gaze fell upon the balloon she had brought her; it was still there swaying from side to side as if waving in a parade. Cali picked up a blue baby rattle that was broken in half and baby clothes that were angrily thrown around. As Cali picked up the clothes she noticed Jena's roommate was looking at her. Her big beautiful brown eyes were filled with unshed tears. Cali had forgotten that quickly she had a roommate.

Folding the little onesie and piling them on the now empty bed, Cali spoke softly, "I'm sorry I forgot you were here. I hope I'm not disturbing you."

She answered quietly, "No, you're not."

Cali probed as she continued picking up baby clothes off of the floor, "Did you know Jena?"

She began to twirl her long red hair around the tip of her middle finger and stared at the floor as she responded, "No, I came in Friday. We just introduced ourselves. She seemed like a nice person when I first got here. I was a little nervous because I'm by myself; my baby's father has not been with me through this pregnancy and she made me laugh. We laughed that whole night and I didn't even think about him. I didn't even know she was going through anything because of how sweet she was towards me. Then, yesterday, we walked to the nursery together to look at our baby's and when we went got there, my baby was there but Jena's baby was not. She asked the nurse to tell her where they had taken her baby. The nurse told her she would have to speak with the doctor. I noticed then how frantic she'd become in just those few seconds." Remembering the drama from the day before made the roommate finally release the tears she'd been holding. As she continued telling Cali everything that happened, it got harder to speak around the heavy golf ball sized lump in her throat. "Jena then asked her why she had to talk to the doctor to see her baby. The nurse had a real attitude. I guess she was getting frustrated with all of Jena's questions and said ma'am, I don't know. I will page him and tell him you want to see him. Jena left to go back to the room alone. When I got back, she was fussing with the guy I figured was the doctor. I didn't want to listen to their conversation so I went into the bath room and took a shower. When I came out of the bathroom, the doctor was gone, but Jena was terribly upset and was crying so uncontrollably I thought her baby had died or something. I asked her did she want to talk about it but she just said it's too late. Nobody can do anything about it now. I didn't know what she was talking about until after she had jumped and some of the other patients were whispering about it."

By this time, they were both in tears. Cali asked while wiping away tears with a tissue and handed one to Jena's roommate, "Did you try to stop her from jumping?"

She shook her head forlornly, "Ma'am, I didn't even hear her get up or knew she'd jumped until it was too late. It was like five o' clock in the morning; I was sleep. I woke up when the nurse brought me my a.m. labs. She knocked on the bathroom door and called for Jena. When she didn't answer she asked me if I'd seen her. I told her, not since last night. That's when she noticed the window was open. She looked out; then screamed. I asked her what the matter was. She ran towards the phone on the wall and said she's down there, she must have jumped. She called for security and after that, all chaos broke loose with all the police and investigators. That's all I know ma'am. I'm still in shock myself. I may even ask to be moved because I don't think I can sleep in this room tonight."

Cali offered, "Would you like me to send someone from my office to talk with you? We can have you moved in a few hours and give any other counseling if you need to just talk. This must be traumatic for you."

She answered with relief, "Yes that will be fine."

Cali stood up to leave but paused, "I am so sorry. I have been talking to you all of this time and I don't even know your name. Please forgive my rudeness."

She shrugged her shoulders as she replied, "My name is Shannon Young."

Cali smiled, "Well, Ms. Young I will have one of my colleagues come and talk with you."

Shannon sounded grateful for her concern, "Thank you."

With all that was going on Cali didn't feel she was the best person to talk with Shannon so she called her colleague Paula Shepherd. Cali stepped out of the room to use the phone at the nurse's station to call Paula to see if she would be available. The news of Jena's suicide traveled fast and Paula accepted Cali's request to speak with her roommate. Cali walked back to the room and told Shannon, "Ms. Paula Shepherd will be up to talk with you and I'll come by and check on you later on or tomorrow, okay?" She offered a reassuring smile and turned to leave. She went back to the nurse's station, this time to ask the nurse to see Jena's file. Cali flashed her badge with authority, but the nurse told her she will have to check with the nurse administrator before releasing them. It took a few minutes for the nurse administrator to call back and confirmed Cali's clearance to see the files. She thanked the nurse on duty and made her way to her office to review the files in privacy.

Cali was eager to find out the name of Jena's doctor. The doctor's name on file was Dr. Peter Martin; it had not dawned on her, that he was her doctor also, because she had always called him dr. P.

Cali called his office to speak with him and was told he was out of town. Cali tried her best to keep the fury out of her voice but it didn't work too well. She wanted to know if he knew his patient had killed herself. His secretary explained he knows, but Doctor Grayson would be handling his cases for right now while he's out of town. The secretary tried to remain cordial but was getting rather impatient with Cali's third degree.

Cali's voice rose a bit, "You mean to tell me, he knew and still went out of town!"

His secretary spoke in his defense. "Ma'am, not that's any of your concern but this business trip, was planned before any of this happened and he could not postpone it."

Cali spoke with a harshness that was uncharacteristic for her, "I wish he had postponed the surgery on her baby instead."

His secretary answered, "Well, that was not a very professional comment"

She retorted, "I'm not feeling very professional right now. And may I ask what floor is Doctor Grayson on?"

She blew into the phone hoping Cali could hear she'd had enough, "Fifth floor. Is that all?" Just as she spouted the last syllable, Cali was so upset she didn't answer her she just hung up. The secretary heard the customary click. She shrugged and went back to her task of updating some files for Doctor Martin.

Cali abruptly stood up. She wasn't sure what she was going to do but she knew she had to do something. She headed for the elevator to go up to the fifth floor but the elevator stopped on the third floor where a couple of interns got on and they were talking about the surgery of the baby and how well it turned out. Cali could not believe what she was hearing; it was like they were bragging about passing a test. When the elevator finally stopped at the fifth floor Cali made her way to exit but stopped short. She turned around and said, "Did you know the mother of that baby killed herself over that surgery you seem to be so proud of?"

The two interns looked stunned as the elevators closed. Cali knew her attitude had been less then professional over these last couple of hours, but she could not shake the disrespect and disregard they had shown towards this mother concerning her child. Cali knocked on the Doctor Grayson's door; he answered in a nice but expectant manner.

His voice, sounded like aged leather, "Come in." He was sitting in a high backed chair, facing his window when he heard her come in. He spun his chair around, smiling as he asked, "How can I help you today?"

Cali paused for a second, noticing his grandfatherly eyes, as to be clear that she heard him correctly because if he was covering for Dr. Martin he had to know already why she'd come. She pressed on; determined to fight for the rights of her dead client. "Dr. Grayson, I'm not sure we've ever met, but I am Dr. Cali Evans of the psychology department. Ms. Jena Sargent was a client of mine, we had an appointment today to discuss something that happened Friday afternoon and I get here this morning and my patient is now dead from an apparent suicide. Dr. Martin was her physician on file and from what I understand is they changed the sex of her baby without her knowledge or consent."

Dr. Grayson answered condescendingly, "We didn't need her consent because her baby was going to be put into foster care anyway."

If it was possible, he would've seen steam escape Cali's ears. "Who told you this? And where is the court documentation backing this."

Dr. Grayson answered with confidence, "I'm sure Dr. Martin has them in his office."

"Don't you think I should have been called if something like this was going to take place? I was listed on her file and I was treating her for a reason. Did you think she was strong enough to go through this or did you all even care? Why was there a rush to change this baby, unless this was a crash course for your interns? Cali fired off questions one by one in her accusatory tone.

Dr. Grayson began stammering now. "What are you talking about?"

Cali politely informed him, "Your interns were just on the elevators talking about it like it was Saturday night football and they score a touchdown. You know what? Never mind, I think I should direct my questions to Dr. Martin when he gets back, because he clearly has not given you enough information for me to close this case."

Dr. Grayson not understand why she's so angry holds his hands up in surrender, "Okay I'm sure he'll get in touch with you when he returns."

He wasn't aware Cali was within hearing distance. As she was leaving she heard him make a call and stated emphatically they will have to silence the program. Cali paused outside of the office and thought, "Silence what program? Are they using babies to give the interns the ability to practice sex changes? Oh God please don't let that be happening."

Chapter 10

When Cali got back to her office it was well past noon. She remembered Lance and agreeing she would have lunch with him if her schedule permitted; being a doctor himself, she was grateful he understood about schedules. Frowning yet the same, she could not see herself clear to eat anywhere and she was thinking she would probably have to also cancel her meeting with Meghan. Her lips were a tight line of tension as she tried to pull her thoughts together.

Just as she was about to pick up the phone to dial Lance's extension; there was a knock on the door. Looking up to see him brought a slow smile to her face. Her eyes sparkled with delight and she found her pulse racing faster at the mere sight of him standing in the doorway. Cali could not have been happier; she came around from behind her desk and hugged him. Relief washed across her shoulders like warm water as she laid her head on his shoulders because she knew when she was with him everything always felt alright. Things hadn't been very good for her since he had dropped her back home for their date. He was surprised she was holding him so long; he felt her distress and knew something was really wrong. With all of her past reservations out of the window, Cali kept whispering in his ear as he held her, "Thank you. Thank you."

It wasn't that he didn't appreciate this new found closeness; but he held himself back to look into her face to find out what had brought this on. With concern he asked, "Cali? What's wrong?" he stroked her back gently as she shuddered against his chest.

She took a deep breath before confiding; "Let's see, where to start?" Her shoulders sagged in defeat as she trusted herself to tell him everything without totally falling apart. "My patient called me this weekend upset. I told her that I would see her this morning, when I got here I found out she'd jumped out the window from the seventh floor."

Lance gasped in surprise, "That was your patient?"

Shaking her head yes, she felt her emotions threaten to cave in. "Yes, she was."

"Oh my God, Cali; I'm so sorry to hear that." He asked, "Do you know why she jumped?"

Anger began to replace her sadness; "All I know is they changed the sex of her baby and she did not want them too or give them the permission."

Stunned, he went on to ask, "Wow, why did they do that?"

Cali tilted her head in dismay, "That's what I have been trying to find out all morning and the doctor that gave authorization to do it is out of town."

Lance figured aloud, "Is this why you have been asking me about sex change?"

She answered, "Yes, I've been dealing with this for a little over a week. I may not have a job after the way I've reacted to all of this."

He frowned, "Why do you say that?"

Her eyes bugged a bit, "I just about accused them of purposely damaging these babies to give their interns practice on sex changing."

Lance settled back into the chair, "Cali you don't have enough information to make this kind of accusation."

Cali couldn't help but to agree but still felt something amiss down in her gut. "I know. You're right, but I just can't believe a sex change was their only option. To do that is going totally against God or our we playing God, I just think our powers should have some boundaries because soon will have people change their babies because that wasn't the sex they wanted or maybe they're already doing that ? Oh my God! What if they are?

Holding his hands up in peace he stopped her before she went any further. Religion and politics were two topics he learned a long time ago to never debate. Lance leaned forward and pushed himself up to leave, "It's okay about lunch; with everything on your mind, I understand you don't have an appetite. I am going to have to get back and finish making my rounds. May I'll cook dinner for you tonight?"

Cali smiled, "I would love for you to make me dinner but tonight I'm going out with Meghan to help her pick out a wedding gown."

Lance stopped short on his way out, "Whaaattt? Meghan is getting married?"

"Yes and she has a little beanie baby in the oven too." Cali answered.

Lance shook his head and smiled along with Cali, "And she's having a baby."

Cali nodded again, "Yes, I know right? My heart gets full just thinking about it."

Lance walked back over to Cali and lifted her chin up to face him. "I know your week hasn't even begun and you have had a lot to deal with, but promise me you will take on only what you can. You know I am here for you and I mean it. If you need me, I don't care what time; I'll be there."

Cali looked at him and seemed to truly see him for the first time and said to herself. "Is this what it feels like to begin falling in love?" He leaned in to kiss her slowly; to his delight, she kissed him back. A surge of desire swept through her chest that surprised both of them. It was this kiss that helped her realize just how strong their attraction was towards one another. Heat gathered between them; they didn't want it to end.

Lance cleared his voice and was the first to totally break away. "Umm, I'll be in my office if you need me."

Cali answered shakily, "Okay."

As soon as Lance closed the door behind him, Cali fell back into her office chair and tried to figure out what just happened to her. Her body was shaking all over, but in a good way. The feelings swirling deeper, bubbling up to the back of her throat made her realize, she'd never felt this way before. Shaking her head, she thought, "Once again Lance came to the rescue."

Lance couldn't escape the cloud of passion that had surrounded them. He made it back to his office on wobbly knees totally mystified at how he had never felt so drawn to a person before as he did towards Cali. He knew he had fallen in love with her and had to have her; he spent the rest of his day wondering if she felt the same.

Cali went to her office bathroom to freshen up. She needed to get her mind back on track; with Jena's case officially closed as far as the hospital was concerned; she had to get in touch with children services to see if she could track down the case manager that may have been working on Jena's file. After meditating for twenty minutes she finally felt calm enough to move on with what her heart was pushing her to do; fight the fight Jena didn't have the strength to contend in. She was passed around to five different people before someone told her the case was given to a Mrs. Destiny Samone. She dialed the number she was given and apprehensively waited for her to answer.

At first Cali thought she was about to get Mrs. Samone's voicemail; just as she was preparing a message to leave a warm voice answered breathlessly. "Hello, Mrs. Samone speaking."

Caught off guard, she cleared her throat before speaking cordially. "Hello Mrs. Samone, this is Dr. Cali Evans. I'm one of the physiologists at West Wood Hospital. I understand you handle Jena Sargent's case? I was calling to find out the status?"

She could hear papers shuffling softly in the back ground and typing as Cali pictured she must have been pulling up all of her case notes and information in her system. "Yes, I was reviewing it earlier and was wondering myself why Jena's baby was going to be placed in foster care since she told me she'd changed her mind and wanted to take care of the baby herself. I spoke with her on Friday. She didn't go into detail of why the people that supposed to have adopted the baby didn't. I explained to her what she needed to do in order to keep her baby. Then I got a call from the hospital's Social Worker saying they need authorization to work on the baby, because he need medical attention and the adopt parent name was on the baby's information as legal guardian this authorization came in Friday right before I was leaving about 4:59PM   Mrs. Samone continued to inform Cali. "Jena has two other children that were placed with the state that I was not aware of until recently. I asked her who had the other two children and she said her mother had them, but her house would have been considered over crowded to place another child.

Cali interjected, "Couldn't they have placed the child temporarily until she could have gotten a job?"

Mrs. Samone answered wholeheartedly, "Ms. Sargent is a bright young woman has the capability to find any job she wants and we still can place the child temporarily until she gets herself on her feet."

Cali was shocked to hear her speak of Jena as if she was still alive. She quickly assessed she must not know that Jena was dead. Cali delved. "When was the last time you spoke with Jena?"

Mrs. Samone calculated the days in her head. "Last Friday; she said she had a boy and wanted to keep him. The hospital social service called and told me the couple who was not interested in adopting and changed their minds."

Cali pressed, "Did she tell you why they changed their mind?"

Mrs. Samone began to wonder where this line of questioning was headed. "No, they didn't. They only said the baby had some undisclosed medical issues that needed to be addressed and would need authorization to act in the best interest of the baby. The director's office sent them authorization forms." By this time Mrs. Samone had had enough answering questions and said, "Dr. Evans evidently you know more about this case than I do. Can you please fill me in?"

Cali sighed inwardly, careful not to allow her anger to show itself, "As a matter of fact, I do, but first I have to tell you that Jena is dead."

In total shock and sadness, Mrs. Samone covered her chest with hand, "She's what?"

Cali repeated, "She's dead Mrs. Samone."

"How did she die? What happened to her?" she asked incredulously.

Cali gathered her emotions enough to explain. "She jumped out of the window of the seventh floor here at the hospital."

Mrs. Samone, still in disbelief, "This is just unbelievable. Why would she do that? She sounded so full of hope when we last spoke." It was hard to keep her feelings out of a case when it came to people like Jena Sargent. Mrs. Samone was deeply saddened to hear she had died. She had a beautiful and loving spirit; life was cruel, but she wasn't an unfit mother, just misguided.

Cali went on with her explanation as Mrs. Samone fought to keep her grief hidden. "The authorization your office sent the hospital gave them permission to change the baby from a boy to a girl and Jena did not want that to happen. As we both know, she was in the process of changing her life around; she wanted to keep her baby. She'd thought God had punished her and she wanted to do better for her family. She was not given that chance. Personally, if I was her I would have hit the roof myself. She was not given any respect at all in this matter from your office or the hospital; this was a young girl that made some mistakes, sure, but she was not on any drugs. She was in labor for nine long hours before they decided to do a "C" section. Nobody was with her and after going through all of that she still was willing to try and give her baby a home with someone that could love him and take care of him. When the adopted parents didn't want any part in it, only a mother could say let me keep my baby the way he was born and no one from your office or the hospital discussed with her what was going to happen to her baby. They treated her as though she did not exist or matter. Jena's last days on this earth could not have been too good because let's please consider everything for a moment." She took a breath and began counting off each point as she continued. "You had a mother with an open wound in her belly, had been held over because she had a high fever, then to find out they changed her baby boy to a girl and to have someone take your child on top of that; to do what they wanted to do to her without her consent? Something is very wrong with this situation." Hearing her no longer able to keep her emotions at bay; Cali realized Mrs. Samone had begun to care for her just as she had. "Look, I'm sorry I had to paint this picture, but I can't help but think about Jena's feeling right know; not yours, mine, or the hospital's"

Mrs. Samone wiped her face with a tissue as she finally spoke up, "I had no idea this had happened. I'm saddened by the death of the client and trust me when I tell you; there will be a full investigation."

Finally, someone concerned for a patient and not just their position and paycheck, Cali thanked her profusely. And before disconnecting the call she asked, "Can you please have Jena's mother contact me? I have some personal items of Jena's and I also want to remind her Jena's now daughter is still in the hospital needing someone to get her."

"Okay, I sure will Dr. Evans. And thank you for enlightening me to this situation. Again, I had no idea any of this was going on. Had I known exactly what the authorization form was for, this never would've happened. And I'll keep you posted on this investigation."

"Before Cali could meet with Megan there was something she had to do, she had to visit Jena's baby. As she gazed thru the nursery window she could see a large baby with a tag saying baby girl Sargent. The baby wasn't given a name. Cali touched the glass window as if to transmit to Jena's baby that his mother loved him. Cali now wondering if she had come at Jena's first call would this have happened? She stood there for about 10 minutes, pondering the thought before returning to her office.

Cali pushed herself to finish updating her paperwork and putting in her report all of the information she'd gathered for the day. She couldn't close it completely in her own system until all information, including the investigation by children services, was complete. Glancing at the clock on her wall she was glad she'd finished in time to meet her best friend. Cali called Meghan to make sure they were still meeting to look for gowns.

Meghan squealed, "Of course! I've been looking forward to this all day!"

Meghan's happiness was infectious, which was what she definitely needed after the emotional roller coaster of day she'd had. Cali smiled into the phone, "I will see you in just a little bit then. I'm shutting everything down so I can leave. Rub the baby for me." Cali was trying to be very careful when talking with Meghan. Because of her pregnancy, she did not want to upset her with everything happening in her work and personal life. After Cali called Meghan she emailed Lance and invited him to dinner for the next day. She chuckled at his quick reply. He'd said, "Yes and who will be cooking?" She hit reply just as quick and typed, "I am cooking; with a smiley face at the end." Lance typed back, "You cook too? I don't know how much more I can take of you. But I thought I'd be the one cooking while you relax ma'am?" Cali loved the amity as she typed back, "Well start exercising, because there is a lot more to me than meets the eye. I will look for you at around six, sir. And next time, you cook." Lance answered, "That sounds good. Do you need me to bring anything?" Cali ended with a flourish, "Nope; just yourself." She closed out of her email box and made her way out of the door feeling balanced and sure for the moment. She pushed all thoughts of Jena to the back of her mind the best she could; to keep it at the forefront would cause an all-out breakdown for sure.

Chapter 11

Cali couldn't wait to see Meghan; readjusting her purse strap on her shoulder, she smiled as she made her way down winding hallways and thought about the catching up and most of all, the planning they had to do. She used the back entrance of the hospital to leave for the day, she did not want to be reminded of the day's events nor did she want to run into anyone who wanted to discuss Jena and any conspiracy theories she was sure had sprung up. She was sure the hospital grapevine crackled with everyone's take on why she committed suicide.

She drove straight to Ruby's and was seated at a table near the window so she could see Meghan when she arrived. She waved excitedly for her to come in when she saw her walk past. Meghan came in like the whirl wind of energy, "Come on, the bridal shop is right down the street."

Cali picked up the menu, "Do we have time for something to eat and a beer?"

Gazing suspiciously as she got comfortable in her seat and placed her handbag beside her, "A beer? Cali, you don't really drink and you want a beer? What's up?"

Cali slumped back in the chair, "I can't talk to you about my issues and all that's going on now because you're pregnant. I don't want you all worried and stressed over me. You and the baby don't need that."

Meghan frowned with a pout, "If you and Doug keep telling me that I am going to scream. I am stronger than you two give me credit for. What happened today? Spill it."

Cali stared at Meghan a moment; giving in. "Meghan, I lost a patient today." She hung her head in sorrow and swallowed hard to keep from crying.

Meghan reached over the table for her hand. "Oh honey, I'm so sorry to hear that; how?"

"She jumped out of the seventh story window today."

Meghan tightened her grip on Cali's hand, "Awl Cali, you've got to be kidding. Oh my God, what was she thinking?"

Cali stuttered, wanting to cut the topic short, "Meg, I can't even talk about this anymore right now; to make this short, they changed her baby boy to a girl without her consent and she jumped. I wanted to talk to you, but now I am going to scream. I need a break from this."

Meghan said, "Cali, I know I brought you to look a gowns and a nice relaxing dinner, but what you really need is a full spa day; the whole shebang kind of spa day; no cell phones or pagers from the hospital."

Cali waved her off, "No let's eat and get your gown." Or" let's get your gown and then eat".

Meghan admonished, "Cali, now don't under estimate your minds need for relaxation. You haven't had time to process that information. You came straight from work to meet me. If you would have had a bubble bath that would have made a little difference but you didn't, please lets go to the spa and get your nails done and your back rubbed and a nice foot bath."

The more things she named, the more Cali thought the spa would be a great idea. She said, "It's sounding better and better. Just the mere thought of a back massage is almost like heaven . . . ."

Meghan laughed and rubbed her belly, "Ewe you nasty girl, I could only imagine where that thought really was headed. You know you want to go too, as she rubbed her belly don't you?"

They laughed and just as they've always done, spoke in unison, "Spa, here we come!"

What started out as a crazy day; ended up being very relaxing. As much as Cali wanted to remember Jena, she knew she had to let the emotional side of it go. She'd learned in college her profession would bring all types of situations and she chided herself for getting emotional with this case. She knew she would have to create a system to be able to purge this type of stress; this time she was using the spa. Cali laid back and relaxed and allowed their time in the sauna and all of the other treatments to absorb her hectic day; she smiled in relief and she had her best friend. The simplicity of it all made her heart fill with gladness.

Cali was the first to break their amicable silence, "Meg, I have some good news."

Meghan sat up anxiously, "Ohhhh, you know I like good news."

Cali could feel herself blush as she admitted, "Lance actually kissed me to day. Girl, he knocked my stockings off! I forgot where we were and I think I knocked his socks off too." She laughed. "He walked away all cool but that kiss was too intense; I just know he felt it.

Meghan clapped excitedly, "It's about time!" Picturing their future she added, "Well if you two get married and have a baby our kids will have each other to play with. They could grow up like cousins!"

Cali inwardly cringed and interrupted her fantasy, "Meghan when I tell you this I don't want you screaming, okay?"

You know I can't make any promises." I get excited.

Cali took a deep breath before telling Meghan something she'd never shared with anyone and said really fast before losing her nerve. "I've never had a period." She shut her eyes and imagined as if Meghan would then say, "Oh you didn't."

Instead, she sat up and took her cucumbers off of her eyes in shock, "You never had a period?"

Cali swallowed hard and began to feel like a specimen underneath a microscope. "No."

Blinking, she thought back through all of the years they'd been best friends. She realized not once did Cali ever complain about bloating and cramps. It never occurred to her. "Well, have you had yourself checked out?" Trying to rationalize this latest secret, Meghan went on to explain; "Cali, you get a period around thirteen years old and you still haven't gotten yours. You used to go to Dr. P, what did he say?"

His only reasoning was I was very athletic and that's the reason I didn't get a period, but I haven't play sports in years. I know something should've happened by now. I did go to another doctor to see about getting a second opinion and when he examined me he asked me if I'd ever had surgery. I told him no; then he wanted me to go to the lab to have some blood work done. After I got dressed and was leaving the examination room they were giving the doctor oxygen; that just freaked me out. When I called the next day, I was told he'd had a stroke." Shrugging, Cali gave her reason for not following up. "I never went back since I had no desire to date and listening to all those girls complaining about their periods, I was in no rush to get mine, so I really didn't miss what I never had and I didn't want to find out something was wrong when I feel perfectly fine." Giving over to her willingness to speak freely now this information was out in the open between them; Cali resumed, "I know if things keep getting serious with me and Lance, I will have to go back and check myself out."

Attempting to change the subject, Cali waved away the look of concern on her best friends face; "Meg, you never told me your colors for your wedding."

Meghan wanted to prolong this conversation concerning Cali never having a period, but if it's one thing she'd learned early on in their friendship it was that when she suddenly changed the subject that meant she was done talking about something. So she didn't push; for now. She found her voice again and tried to act as if they hadn't just discussed something so serious. "I like fuchsia and purple and my gown will be an ivory color."

Cali began smiling broadly as she imagined the colors and how the church would look, "That will beautiful. Tell me more Meghan. It seems like every time we talk it is mainly about me and my issues, so how are things with you and Doug? I know you're getting married and you're having a baby but are you really happy?"

Meghan answered confidently, "I'm very happy! Doug is very good to me! Cali you should know that I wouldn't have slept with him if he wasn't. Doug will make a great father and a great husband or I may just have to kill him."

Cali stared closely at Meghan to see how serious she was. They burst into laughter.

"Girl you are crazy!" Cali yelped and tried to gather herself. "You remember that day we went to The Topple? You were having such a good time and by the way I didn't know you danced so good; I'd prayed that you would find someone to make you happy, you so deserve it."

Meghan felt herself tear up. She hugged Cali close and said, "I wish the same for you."

Cali announced after they'd both settled back into lounging in the sauna; "I've invited Lance over for dinner tomorrow and I have to find something spectacular to cook."

Meghan added, "Speaking of cooking, I need to get home and fix dinner. Do you believe Doug truly likes my cooking?"

Laughing along with her, Cali said, "Now that's love."

Meghan made a face, "Ha, Ha, Ha; okay Ms. Betty Crocker. I'll remember that when you want look sexy on that next date."

*****

The next day Cali decided to work from home; she wanted to do some research on new born sex changes and find out how life has been for those children. She figured this type of procedure had to have been going on more than the normal public could even know. She felt sure this has left some children with identity problems where you sometimes see them on shows like Jerry Springer and other shows that sometimes make these kids look like freaks or to others as living immorally wrong. Some of them yelling out to anyone who would listen; I don't feel right in this body and they're sometimes disowned by family and friends. So far, she'd learned from her research only boys were being changed sexually but she had yet to come across this happening to girls born to parents who wanted boys and changed them.

Cali was putting these questions out there for more feedback and dialogue. She wrote an editorial and called the topic Children of Change. She emailed it to the editor of the New York Dailey Times. Cali finally took a break from her work; her eyes were tired from reading article after article on her computer screen. She took a moment to notice the time and knew she had only a few hours to get ready for dinner with Lance, so she finished her editorial and pressed send. Cali had been wanting information on this since she'd first heard of it and was nervously hoping her editorial would be posted.

Cali glanced at her watch again and saw she had less than three hours to get ready for her dinner with Lance. She decided on something simple but good for dinner; her go-to menu of t–bone steaks, her favorite tri- pasta salad, and glazed peaches for dessert; she fired up the grill. As the coals readied themselves, she quickly marinated two large steaks and straightened up around her home. Being the neat freak she was; it wasn't much that needed to be done but she wanted to freshen up the area anyway. After taking her shower Cali slipped into a soft silky peach sun dress and pearl earrings. She knew blue was Lance's favorite color, but peach was hers. She found she didn't have to do much to herself because of the wonderful spa treatments she'd enjoyed with Meghan. It'd left her feeling better and her skin was glowing; only a little mascara and lip gloss were needed to complete the summery carefree look she was going for.

She set the patio table with a peach table cloth and white candles in gold candle holders. Even though it was outside she pulled out her finest China; a house warming gift from her mother; white iridescent pearl plates. The lightly vanilla-lavender scented candle light made them sparkle. The weather was warm and balmy with a soft breeze; a perfect evening for eating outside. Cali placed the steaks on the grill whose coals were snow white and ready for cooking and finished setting everything on the table with the salad. She was saving the glazed peaches for dessert, so she left them on warm in the oven. The final touch was soft music; Kenny G was added to the menu. As she went about finishing up her tasks, Cali made up her mind to finally let Lance know how she felt.

Just as she was giving a satisfying look over her set table she heard the doorbell ring. It was Lance; she checked herself in the mirror, took a deep breath, and opened the door. They took each other in with satisfaction and surprise as she observed Lance was wearing light beige khaki pants and a peach colored polo shirt. They shared a laugh of how this was the second time they were on a date and matched each other. She welcomed him with a hug and beckoned him to come in and make himself at home. Feeling him this close after their kiss caused a soft heat to build in the pit of her belly as she noted something else with Lance she'd never given notice to before; his shirt clung to his chest showing he did indeed work out. She all of sudden had the urge to run her fingers down the front of his shirt to feel his muscles ripple beneath her touch. Cali had to shake herself out of the reverie; this only confirmed her knight in shining armor was definitely buff.

He complimented her; told her she looked beautiful and handed her a bouquet of baby breath flowers. She took them and put them in a vase and set them out on the table; she smiled as she realized it gave her setting that final touch.

She asked, "Would you like some wine?"

He answered with a smile of his own, "Yes." When she brought his wine to him he leaned in and kissed her. She smiled and took his hand and led him to her patio outside. He gave accolades to her on her nicely decorated patio garden. He sniffed the air while taking a seat, "Is that steak I smell?"

Cali answered, "Yes it is."

"You mind if I check on them?" He asked as he began to stand.

"Not at all, I'll go grab the rest of the wine."

"Okay." Lance answered as he opened the grill and turned the steaks. "You sit and relax; I'll take over from here."

When she came back through the door, he pulled out her chair for her to sit. He grabbed each plate and placed the steaks off of the grill. He grabbed the salad tongs and added some to each plate. Cali couldn't stop herself from smiling. He was so endearing and was always taking care of her in some kind of way. After refilling their glasses with wine he sat down to join her. They made a toast to a wonderful evening and promised work would not be on the menu.

As they ate and discussed everything but work; Cali heard her favorite Kenny G song. She began to sway back and forth. Lance stood up and reached for her hand to dance. Cali didn't hesitate as she'd done before; she knew how to follow him. He held her tighter than he did before and Cali didn't mind one bit. She relished in the feeling of being close to him; the smell of his cologne and the feel of his hand in the small of her back. When they finished dancing they took their wine glasses and sat in Cali's cozy two seated lounge wicker chair. He took a swallow from his glass and slowly turned to face Cali.

Cali stared longingly at him as he prepared to speak. He held on to her hands and caressed the top of her hands with his thumbs. "Cali, I have a confession to make. I'm falling in love with you. When I'm not with you I find myself wondering what you're doing. I know you said you didn't want to rush into things but I want us to be a couple." Her silence made him nervous. She had no idea how his heart beat so fast anticipating her answer. Hooking Cali was tougher than any fish he'd ever tried to catch. He watched her face for any signs of a let-down as he waited for her to answer.

Cali dropped her head and told herself it was now or never. Since he was laying his heart on the line she would too and finally take a chance at happiness. "Lance, I'd like that very much. Here I was all ready to give this speech I've been practicing in my head all day but you made it easy for me."

He laughed with relief as he pulled her into his embrace. This time when they kissed she knew for sure his socks were knocked off. If kissing felt this good she wasn't sure if she was so ready for anything else at the moment. It felt like her heart was beating out of her chest as he explored the hollow of her neck with soft intimate kisses. For the rest of the evening they relaxed in the lounge chair in each other's arms. It was going on three o' clock in the morning when Lance was first to wake; he hated to disturb her peaceful rest but he gently shook her to tell her he was going home. Cali was tempted to tell him he could just stay and hold her but she knew where that would possibly lead to. She moaned and stood to walk him to the door. He was kind of hoping she'd ask him to stay but didn't want to push his luck. Instead he spoke tenderly in her ear, "Go on and enjoy your bed. Tomorrow is another day on the battlefield at the hospital. You need your rest." They shared another passionate kiss that almost made him forget about pushing his luck. "I'll talk to you later."

Cali shut and locked the door as regret replaced the euphoria she'd just been experiencing. For the first time she'd wanted a man for more than just a friendly game of basketball. Cali dragged herself to bed. As her head found it's favorite spot on the pillow she thought to herself, Lance didn't know just how lucky he was about to be.

Chapter 12

It was about eight a.m. when Cali made into her office. She really didn't feel like being there because it reminded her of Jena. She noticed she had several messages to return; one of them she was very surprised to see was from Jena's mother asking questions about what happened to her and wanting to know the whereabouts of her grandchild. Cali had never heard Jena talk about her mother, but now she knew there were a lot of things Jena didn't talk about. Before she could get herself together to return any of her calls, her line rang disturbing her thoughts. It was Jena's mother; Cali could not wait to hear the reason for her absence during Jena's stay in the hospital. Cali answered her call and set up a meeting for two o'clock that afternoon. To take her mind off of Jena Cali decided to check on her personal email messages and was excited she had a return e-mail from the Dailey Times of New York letting her know they chose her article to publish. They also offered her a guest spot on their local show to speak on that topic, but she declined, she felt she knew absolutely nothing on the subject of baby sex changes. She explained in her response her main reason for writing the article was to get feedback hopefully from a doctor that has performed this type surgery or from any patient or family member that has lived through this type of surgery. After she e-mailed them back; she received another e-mail; it was from the hospital administrator letting her know there would be a four o'clock meeting regarding Jena Sargent's death. This meeting was definitely something she was not looking forward to, but she had to close her file with the hospital's investigation report.

She utilized the rest of her time to drop by and check on her other clients and was relieved to find everyone else was doing fine. After visiting her last patient, Cali decided to stop by Lance's office to see if he had time for lunch. He said closing the file he'd been reviewing, "Sure am. I'm hungry too. I'll be ready in five minutes."

Instead of hospital cafeteria food they held hands and made their way to eat at a small diner down the street. Enjoying the sunshine they strolled along the sidewalk and enjoyed each other's company. Cali filled Lance in with how the hospital administration called a meeting for four o'clock that day.

"This sounds important. What do they want to meet about? It must be pretty serious for the admins to get together."

She went on to explain; "Jena Sargent's case."

He snapped his fingers, "Yea that's right. Are you nervous?"

Cali thought a second, "No, I don't have anything to be nervous for, but on the other hand it will be interesting to see how they will wiggle their way out of this. I just can't see them saying they're at fault."

Lance gave his opinion, "Well can you really blame them? I am speaking from a financial aspect of it; they could be sued for millions so you know they will be pulling out their big guns to keep that from happening."

Cali nodded, "Yea, I totally agree and I forgot to tell you I also have an appointment with her mother at 2:00pm."

Lance held her hand tighter and played with her fingers, "Have you spoken with her mother before?"

Cali shook her head no and mentioned, "She had a lot of questions when she called. She didn't know the whereabouts of her grandchild and I don't think she has much information on what happened to Jena either. I'll be seeing her before I meet with the hospital and Lance I swear I will not do their dirty work for them. At this point I cannot and will not speak on anything because I have to receive the hospital's final report so I will direct her to their office and let them be the bearer of bad news."

Lance opened the door to the deli as he said, "Honey, I agree. I don't blame you one bit."

Cali and Lance enjoyed their lunch and headed back to the office. Before they made it to hospital premises Lance stopped Cali with a look she was becoming accustomed to; he took her into his arms and gave her a mind blowing kiss. So caught up in each other, they were a few minutes late returning from lunch but neither minded as they waved good-bye to one another and went about finishing their work day.

As Cali approached her office she eyed a very attractive fair skinned lady waiting outside her door. They looked each other eye to eye before saying anything. The lady asked, "Are you Dr. Evans?"

Cali glanced at her watch, "Yes I am."

The lady answered, "I'm Jena's mother. I had a two o'clock appointment with you and I know I'm early; I hope you don't mind."

She waved away her worries as she opened her office to let her go in. "No, that's fine. I thought I'd misunderstood the time you'd requested to meet is all." Cali walked in behind her and added, "Please have a seat. I'll be right with you."

Cali put her purse away and quickly checked her e-mail. She finally came out to join Mrs. Sargent in her waiting area. Cali didn't want to appear to be cold or unemotional concerning Jena's death, but she knew she couldn't keep going on these emotional rides. She plainly came out and asked Mrs. Sargent, "How may I help you today?" Hoping this way it would let Cali know just how much information her mother knew without volunteering any herself.

Mrs. Sargent softly cleared her throat and sat back in her seat, she began by saying, "I know you were Jena's psychologist. One of the last times I spoke to my daughter she'd decided to give her baby away.

I argued with her about her decision because I wanted her to change her life around. I have her other two children.

Cali interrupted, "You have her other two children? I thought they were with the state?"

Mrs. Sargent explained, "They say the babies are with the state because they were placed in my home just like any other foster care case, but I just so happened to be the grandmother. They send me money for taking care of her children and I would have taken care of the baby, but I didn't have enough room with the way the law states how many people can be to a room and I didn't want to move. I have been living in my home for over twenty years and I know everyone there and they know me. If something goes wrong I know who to call and who I can depend on." She took a moment to compose herself before speaking any further. "That's why I was trying to make Jena keep this baby because I didn't want my grandchild separated from her sister and brother.

Cali asked before she could stop herself, "What about the father?"

Mrs. Sargent pursed her lips in disappointment; "He's just as bad off as Jena and every time he came around Jena would threaten she'd call the welfare people on him for child support. That would make him leave real fast." She continued. "Dr. Evans, Jena wasn't always in a bad situation. She used to get all A's in school but when she got into junior high she changed. Jena had a sister a little older than her and a younger brother, but she had the darker complexion of my three children. The oldest is fair colored like me and the youngest is just a shade darker than me but Jena turned out dark like her dad so by the time she got in junior high she was teased per se by her siblings; even doubting they were sister and brother and of course like siblings tend to do when they would get mad at her they would tell her "that's why mommy adopted you", but Dr. Evans Jena never ever knew she was my favorite. She was very compassionate and always made sure I was okay when I was sick." Remembering her sweet baby girl, it became hard to speak, but she found the courage to go on. "Jena took care of me. And when it came to those kids, I don't know how she got the money but she always made sure they had new up to date clothes and a beautiful Christmas; of course that's something the state did not care about. The only difference with her situation is those children did not live with her, but she was still a good mother. She still came by every night to bathe them and read to them before bedtime and the fact she was dark reminded me so much of their father." She began to cry.

Cali offered her the tissue box and fought back her own tears. She found strength to continue, "Dr. Evans I just want to know what happened to her and where they took my grandbaby."

The straight forward answer she'd planned on giving went totally out of the window by the time Jena's mother had finished. Momentarily at a loss of words, Cali had to push her emotion away, "Mrs. Sargent, there's still an investigation on the matter. I was not there so I don't even know what happened but I can tell you this, she was going to keep her baby and she had spoken of turning her life around for the better."

Mrs. Sargent sniffed and reached for another tissue, "Thank you for taking time out of your busy day to speak with me Dr. Evans."

Cali smiled sadly, "Mrs. Sargent, I don't want you leaving here with so many unanswered questions but the hospital has a patient services department that can probably answer your questions better than I can at the moment. I think you need to speak with someone about your daughter's death; that should get them moving and you should get a lawyer to make clear some things you may not understand."

They both stood. Mrs. Sargent thanked Cali again as she was pointed in the direction of patient services. After watching Mrs.

Sargent make her way solemnly down the hall, Cali returned to sit at her desk to reflect on their meeting; even though it was very sad, Cali was glad it turned out the way it did. She had a better understanding of who Jena really was as a mom and a daughter. The file she'd received the day she'd become her patient portrayed her as a dead beat mom. Cali knew for sure she was truly the sweet Jena she remembered talking to. Cali went over Jena's files again to make sure she hadn't left anything out. She knew after this meeting with the upper echelon of hospital administration Jena's file would be closed. She reviewed the file until it was time to go to her meeting.

As Cali approached the administration office she heard people talking.

She knocked on the door. Someone answered, "Come in."

When she walked in she noticed she was not the only one called to the meeting; along with the administrator there was Dr. Baines and to her surprise, her doctor Dr. P.

The surprise apparent in her voice, she said, "Hi Dr. P, what are you doing here?"

He was just as surprised to see her and answered with the same, "Cali, what are you doing here?"

She said while searching the pockets of her lab coat for an ink pen, "Jena Shepherd was my patient."

A big wind must have blown down his throat; he started to get all choked up and started reaching for some water. Not knowing what was going on, she asked, "Dr. P, are you okay?"

He managed, "Yes, I'll be fine." Dr. P had not seen Cali since she was about fifteen years old, he did not know if her parents told her about herself, but here she was upset about her patient's baby being changed and he's at the footnote of it all.

When the hospital director came in he asked for everyone to have a seat. Cali was still trying to figure out why Dr. P was there; that is until the director called him Dr. Martin. Cali swayed and almost fell out of her chair. Forgetting all decorum, Cali piped incredulously, "Dr. P, you're Dr. Martin."

He cleared his throat again and sweat began to gather around his collar and under his arms. "Yes."

She questioned, "And you gave permission for the surgery on Jena's baby?"

Not really wanting to say anything further, he found the nerve to speak, "Yes."

The administrator listened intently to this exchange as Cali didn't let up, "So, it was you I was trying to get in contact with?"

Knowing good and well it was her who'd been hounding his office about this baby, he was still cautious with his answers. "Yes, I think so."

Cali shook her head and said, "This is unbelievable." To think her child hood doctor was partly to blame for her patient's death. Cali quickly scanned over the investigation summary report the administrator had handed to them on his way in to take a seat and after reading it she completely lost her cool. "You mean to tell me a mother does not have the right to tell the hospital what they can or cannot do with their baby they gave birth to?" Her body visibly shook with anger. "That mother, my patient said she did not want her baby's gender changed."

Dr. Baines interjected, "It was never written that she didn't want it changed."

Cali yelled, "She told me! And it's noted in her files that she was keeping her baby the way he was! Mighty strange how all of the nurses knew; her roommate too; it seems like everyone knew except you guys!"

The director, a balding middle aged gentleman; eight months from retirement wiped his face with his handkerchief and tried to gain control of the meeting. "Dr. Evans, the baby was in the hands of the state and they sent us an authorization to do the surgery."

Cali not caring about the repercussions boldly stated, "Well, you had better take this investigation report back to the drawing board because I spoke with the case worker for Jena and they were not aware of a gender change for that baby. They were only told the baby needed some medical treatment done. You took the time to call for authorization for a gender change, but you didn't inform them their patient killed herself; which also means this patient's death was left for two days without family being notified; now the state is doing their own investigation."

Cali asked both doctor's, "Did any of you think through your slicing and dicing that the baby's mind would function as a boy?" They shared a look of bewilderment. She carried on, being the voice Jena no longer had. "No, I don't think you did." Cali took off her badge and slammed it on the desk. In the few minutes it took to say all she had to say she'd made up her mind she no longer wanted her job. "Consider this my resignation." She stood proudly; feeling better about her rash decision as each second ticked by. "Good day, director, Dr. Baines." With a drawn, hurt look she faced Dr. Martin, "And oh by the way, Jena's mother was here to see me today. I'm glad I advised her to get a lawyer. Wiggle yourself out of this one." She slammed the door on her way out. Dr. P avoided eye contact with Cali because he knew she now knew his role in the case; his heart thudded at her words; he felt the end of his illustrious medical career was fast approaching.

Cali marched back to her office with a feeling of vindication as she typed her official resignation. She was so fed up with everything that she called for their inter-office courier to take it to the administration office. In the midst of dialing Lance's extension she immediately changed her mind; she did not want to call him with this drama. It seemed as though since she's known him it has been all about her and the issues she's been dealing with. She had no idea what Lance went through being he never complained to her about anything; so she resolved to honor him with the same. She was tired of having a negative conversation to greet him with.

She wasn't sad about leaving her job; as a matter of fact, she felt a sort of relieved. She did wonder how Lance would feel when she did tell him about her decision. Would she look negative in his eyes? Giving herself an inner pep talk; she smiled as she thought she had to do what was right for her. Money wasn't an issue either because she never really went anywhere or spent frivolously, so she had a nice savings to hold her over until she decided her next career move.

There was only one box Cali had to pack up with her things. She carried it out to the car; each step feeling lighter as she neared the parking garage. She pressed the open button of her keyless entry, the lights blinked quickly. Placing her box on the back seat; she didn't even look back. As Cali pulled off she felt such a freedom she opened her windows and yelped a cry of release and allowed it to be carry over the wind as she made her way down the road. It wasn't until she felt the dampness on the front of her shirt she realized she'd been crying. Sitting at a red light, she glimpsed herself in the rearview mirror, shook her hair out of her ponytail, smiled, and sped off with a new found peace.

Chapter 13

She found herself driving straight to Meghan's new house; it was time to take her to pick out her wedding gown. This would be her first visit; she thought back to when they first graduated college they both lived in apartments but since finding out about the baby she and Doug purchased a new home. Cali couldn't believe how beautiful everything was as she drove through the neighborhood; manicured lawns perfect enough for any home and garden magazine. It was in a gated community; she had to be buzzed through the gate. As she drove winding road towards their driveway, Cali took in the view. There were fish ponds on both sides of the road, peach trees, roses; you name it, they had it and it was strategically landscaped to the appearance of an English countryside.

When she reached the door Meghan yanked the door open. They screamed, kissed, and hugged as if they hadn't seen each other in years instead of just a few days ago. They just couldn't get enough of each other.

Cali exclaimed as she took in the foyer, "Meghan, this house is goooooooorgeous! What does you future husband do again for a living? You sure it's legal?" Laughing, Meghan pulled Cali further into the house. The spiral steps were to die for with mahogany wood; the marble floors with spacious kitchen made Cali's head swim with dreams of her own palatial home front someday. Cali continued her semi self-tour, "Meg! You didn't tell me about the pool!"

Megan smiled, "I was saving that tidbit for last. Picture it, the both of us looking sexy this summer pool side with umbrellas in our drinks." They high fived; Cali followed her friend into the den. "Now that we have that out of the way; I know you. What's going on? And what do you want to drink?"

Cali sat back comfortably in the chaise lounge she spotted from the door, "You know me, bring me a beer." She crossed her feet beneath her body and prepared to rehash her life since last seeing Meghan. "Where should I start?"

Megan poured an ice cold beer into a glass and glanced over her, Okay, at the beginning."

Cali exhaled. She figured she'd talk about the good first. "Okay, I had a good time with Lance last night."

She handed her the glass and took a seat on the sofa; with an eyebrow arched inquired. "Did you; now?"

Swallowing her fist sip, Cali shook her head simultaneously, "No, I didn't mean in that way, nasty girl."

Meghan shrugged, "Now that's love."

Laughing, she continued, "Well Lance told me he's in love with me. I told him I feel the same so we're on point, but I got to work I had a voicemail from Jena's mother who wanted to meet with me at two o'clock and another meeting with the hospital concerning the Jena's case was at four o' clock." Cali took another swallow from her beer, "I met with her first; very beautiful woman who looks nothing like Jena. But I found out she has Jena's children and didn't have enough room for the other child or they would make her move out of the house she's been living in for over twenty years. Of course, she didn't want to move and she'd been fighting with Jena to get herself together so the children would not be separated. She was against the adoption and had no idea about the baby's gender change. I didn't tell her or the reason Jena died." Meghan's hormones were giving her fit; she fought back tears as she listened intently. "She told me some of the reasons that led to Jena getting out of whack but overall she was a good mother." Cali took a moment to drink some more beer. "I was happy to hear that."

Meghan asked, "Well, how did she find out about the baby?"

Cali shook her head again, "She still didn't know although she may know by now, but I pointed her towards patient services. I feel like they should be the ones to be the bearer of bad news and then this is the kicker!" Meghan sat forward as though she may miss a word being said. "At my meeting with the hospital guess who was there?"

Who? Meghan frowned. "Lance?"

"Dr. P." she answered.

Meghan screamed, "Shut up! What the heck was he there for?"

Cali took one long drink before continuing, "Listen to this; he's the Dr. Martin on the   paperwork."

Meghan was almost standing at this news, "The doctor who gave permission for the surgery?"

"Yes; the one and the same." Cali answered.

Meghan's mind was working overtime. "But how is it you didn't know?"

"Think about it . . . what have I always called him? Dr. P. I never knew his name was Peter Martin."

Meghan nodded in understanding, "Oh my God Cali, what did you do?"

Cali sat up herself, getting hyper herself all over again, "I QUIT!! Now let's go get our dresses. I'll tell you the details of the meeting another time about what I said but trust me I gave them a lot to think about. Besides, I've wanted to go into private practice anyway. I was tired of that little rat trap they called an office and you know I have enough money for at least a couple of years, so let's go."

Meghan wanted to know. "That's all good and I'm happy for you, but wait, does Lance know?"

Cali replied with hopes of getting no further questions, "No, let's go." She grabbed Meghan's hand and led her out of the front door. Cali wanted Meghan to be comfortable, "Is the car seat back far enough?" Meghan smiled and decided to enjoy the extra attention instead of fussing about it all of the time. "Where are we going first?"

Meghan suggested, "Let's go to that boutique down the street from Ruby's Diner where we were trying to go to before? The name is Mead's Fashion Boutique."

Blasting the radio, the two best friends rode back into town. Meghan smiled over at the woman who has been like a sister to her. She did seem more care-free but there was something still lurking behind her heart; she wished she knew what it was so she could help. Catching her staring, Cali smiled back, reached over and rubbed her hand over Meghan's belly in appreciation. Their bond didn't need words. By the time they made it downtown they were dancing in their seats and giggling like old times.

Meghan tried on five wedding gowns before she finally found one she absolutely loved; a cream colored vintage Vera Wang with pearl accents on the bodice; it had a slight flare to camouflage her pregnancy; she just hoped her belly would remain its current size until after the ceremony. She didn't want to try on anything else or have to re-size her entire dress at the last minute. With the bride satisfied; they found Cali's dress; a knee length fuchsia colored cocktail dress with an empire waist that flattered Cali's boyish figure immensely. Cali twirled around in the double mirror admiring the way she looked in the dress, she couldn't stop smiling; picturing herself all made up for the big day with a nice up-do and light make-up. Her feelings were highly infectious; Meghan and the boutique owner smiled along with her as she pranced around their make shift catwalk.

The same boutique also had an extensive brochure of flower arrangements and even supplied a vendor for wedding cakes, they were able to browse and order the flowers, but the decision for the wedding cake, grooms cake, and food was left up to Meghan and Doug. With the shopping done, the lady with the growing belly was hungry. She suggested they go back to Ruby's Diner to get some shrimp. Cali agreed, "That sounds good!" They shared a basket of shrimp, sweet tea, and easy conversation.

*****

After Cali dropped Meghan at home, she called Lance; he answered his office line after the second ring, "Hi."

"Hey yourself, what a nice surprise; I've wanted to hear your voice all day."

Cali blushed at his sentiment. "That's sweet Lance. I was calling because I need to see you."

He organized some lab work he'd been reviewing and paused at the seriousness of her voice. "Would you like me to stop by your office? I'm done with everything for the day. I could stop by on my way out."

Shaking her head as if he could see her through the phone, she answered, "No, I am home."

Hearing she was at home made him sit up straight in his chair with deeper concern, "Are you all right?"

She replied, "Yes, I'm fine. Just stop by when you get off."

"Okay, I'll be on my way in about ten minutes." Hanging up the phone, Lance frowned with concern, trying to figure out what it could possibly be she had to speak with him about. He remembered she had to meet with the hospital administration today and wondered how it turned out. He figured that is what she wanted to talk about. After making one last round, he moved with an extra pep in his step and could not wait to see his Cali. He had something to ask her as well; his heart skipped a few beats with anticipation.

The drive seemed farther than usual. He had to make himself slow down to keep from getting a ticket or worse. He chuckled to himself as he resolved it was just the desire to be in her presence that had him all anxious. He tried to calm his nerves as he waited for her open the door; he heard movement within. The door opened and there stood Cali, looking freshly showered in a pair of lounging pants and a t-shirt. Her face shined with an inner glow and her lips were lightly glossed. He leaned in to her welcoming arms and lingered in the doorway with a kiss. Then stood back to inspect before asking again, "Are you sure you're okay? You sounded kind of serious on the phone." He was looking at her body as if he was looking for body injuries.

Grabbing his hand and pulling him into the living room; she sat him down and kissed him again. "I called you because I wanted you to hear this from me instead of the hospital gossip line. Today, I quit my job."

"Wow." He asked for details. "Did something happen at the meeting?" He sat back and made himself comfortable.

Before getting into everything she offered him a drink. He nodded yes and waited for her to return with some wine. Cali sat back down and picked up where they left off by answering his question. "Yes, but I quit on my own. They did just what we expected them to do; Lance when I looked around that table and heard how they were trying to cover things up, it made me sick. I no longer wanted to be a part of that team. Besides, I've always planned to go into a private practice anyway. Now is as good as any to make that happen."

He appreciated her tenacity. "I'm proud of you Cali for taking a stand for your patient. Have you started looking for a space yet?"

"Not yet." She answered as she ran her hands through her hair. "I'm still wrapping my head around everything. But I will be looking for something spacious with windows all around to let the sun shine in. I feel so free just thinking about it everything I want to do from here on out." She paused to look at him. She loved taking in his features. His strong chin, deep set thoughtful eyes that pulled you in with a glance; his nose full and prominent fit his chiseled chin.

Lance broke the silence, "I have a question to ask you. I purchased two tickets last week, they are open ended so I can go at any time but, the destination choices would be the Bahamas, Aspen or Hawaii. I know this is on short notice, but I am going on vacation next week and I would like for you to go with me."

Cali stared thoughtfully before giving her answer. "Lance; that is something I don't do; going away with men."

"I assure you we will have separate sleeping quarters." Lance felt honored she was not the type of woman who didn't want to rush into bed. He'd been down that road before and it left him alone. His relationship with Cali was one that moved as slow as molasses and he loved every moment of it. He didn't want to rush into things as he'd done before.

Cali leaned forward to pour them another glass of wine. "That does sound nice and this would be the perfect time to get away. I don't have anything else to do; look I just quit my job." She shrugged and smiled happily. "Yes Lance, I would love the go."

Taking a drink of his wine he asked, "Well, where are we going? Bahamas? Aspen? Hawaii?"

"Hmmm;" Bouncing her foot up and down as she decided. "Bahamas, but I just have one question." She cut her eyes at him. "How did you know I would say yes?"

They shared a laugh. "I didn't." Being honest with his response, he continued. "I was hoping."

She took a pillow from her chair and hit him with it. He pulled her down on the couch with him and kissed her. He knew the romance was fully in bloom. He stopped kissing her long enough to say; "So, will taking next week off be okay for you?"

Cali smiled, "Of course, whenever you want to is fine with me. It's not like have anything else planned."

Lance was so excited he called the airport from Cali's house and gave them the departure date.

Chapter 14

The next day Lance called one of his realtor friends and told him he was looking for an office suite. He requested he wanted the top floor and it must be a corner lot with windows and decorated too. He explained he wouldn't be able to look at anything he had to show due to being out of town the next week, but wanted it finished by the time he returned. He also requested pictures be sent to him and he will tell them her favorite colors and her decorative taste. His plan was to surprise Cali with her office was falling into place. He smiled as he placed his phone back into its base. Lance also went to a jeweler and purchased a princess cut ten carat diamond ring. He had another question to ask and he had high hopes Cali would say yes to that one too.

For the first time Cali went by herself to buy some clothes at the mall; not those pant suits she usually wore, but she ventured into other choices of sexy women's clothing. Any other time she wouldn't hesitate to call Meghan to help her; even feeling as if; at times; it was Meghan's civil duty to help her. Not this time; she felt like she was coming into her own person. She wanted to look good for Lance all on her own and besides how hard can it be to say yes to something that looked good or no it doesn't? The first thing she purchased was a bathing suit; a one piece halter top, blue with vertical white stripes. She also noticed another one she liked; this one, a zebra print one piece tube top. She'd eyed a few bikinis but cringed at the thought of how she'd look in them. Even though Meghan was kind enough as her friend to tell her she could wear almost anything, she would not push the envelope in wearing a two piece. She knew her style limits and didn't want to be the woman other people talked about; thinking she was cute when she really looked an awful mess.

Next, she went to buy a couple of casual outfits. She fell in love with a white goddess shear lined dress, trimmed in gold; of which, she thought would be for an evening out. Two sun dresses and sandals rounded out her shopping, she knew if she needed anything else she could buy it in the Bahamas. There is, one thing she'd almost forgotten; she noticed the lingerie section as she made her way out of the store. She made a left and to browse through some sexy undies. She knew as a woman granny pantie's was a no-no even though Cali found them very comfortable; for this trip she'd go sexy all of the way. She grinned stupidly as she was sure Lance would love her in anything she put on but she didn't want to push it. She gave in to some sexy thigh highs, thongs would have taken her to a level she was not ready for.

Cali was pooped when she'd finished shopping. Her eyes were so heavy by the time she pulled into her driveway. She went home and took a nice hot bath and poured herself a glass of wine. She always indulged in lots of bubbles. Cali laid back and enjoyed her bath and wine; she thought of her life and was glad she was finally in a place of no more regrets. No more feeling like woe is me. She sat and thought of all the things she had to be happy for. Sure, she had just quit her job, but she still had so much to be thankful for. Starting with the fact she had a friend she couldn't have wished for who had been so great, who had been her parachute as she'd flown helplessly at times, who had been her lighthouse when she was in the dark, and who had showed her love before she even knew what love was; a love that had blocked so many fiery darts that she never saw; God had truly sent her a gift and that was Meghan.

And when she'd thought that was enough, God sent her this diamond; just a speck and she watched each day as that sparkle got brighter and brighter, now it's a star, she thought as she allowed the wine to take effect. Salt from her tears now mixed with the wine as she mumbled aloud, "He sent me Lance and he continues to light up my life." She toasted herself as she continued to ponder. Oh yeah she had a lot to be thankful for. Cali emerged herself in her bath, taking herself under like she was baptizing herself. When she came up she felt like a new person ready to live her life to the fullest.

The next morning when the alarm didn't sound off Cali awakened with a jolt thinking of how late she was going to be. She stopped herself just as she was about to jump about of bed and take a shower. She remembered she didn't have a job to go to so instead she made a hair appointment to get some high lights. Her favorite salon gave her one for two o' clock that afternoon. Even though Cali had a spa treatment just a few days before, she was so ready for another pedicure; glancing down and wiggling her toes she talked to herself, "Well at least a polish change." She didn't need an appointment for that so she got herself up so she could get ready to make her way to the nail shop, her usual shop where she could walk right in. After she took a shower, dressed, and enjoyed a cup of coffee; she checked her e-mail and was surprised but flattered to see a message from the administrator. He told her he would hold her resignation until after the weekend. He realized she was upset about her patient and if after a couple days off maybe she would reconsider. And if he hadn't heard from her by noon on Monday then he would have no choice but to summit it to H.R. Her next message was even more pleasing than the first; it was from the New York Daily Times. They told her that the feedback on her article had been unbelievable and they were sending her the complete article along with the responses.

Cali finished getting dressed and left her house in an awesome mood as she went to get her pedicure. While she was there she called Meghan. "Guess where I am?"

Meghan laughed, "Where are you Cali?"

She smiled at the attendant massaging her legs and said, "I am getting my feet done."

Meghan couldn't understand why she was giddy over getting another pedicure. "Umm, you had them done the other day. Didn't you like it?"

Cali could tell she was wondering what had her in such a good mood. "Yes, but this is for a special occasion."

Hearing this made Meghan's ears perk up; "Oh yeah? What's going on?"

"You're not going to believe this but first let me tell you this tidbit; the administrator sent me an e-mail saying he's holding my resignation until noon Monday hoping this weekend is giving me some cooling off time."

"I think that's great they still want you. They know what they have in you. So, are you going back?"

Cali's ,Heck no, Meg I feel so good leaving there and it makes me sick to even think of going back. That's why I know I did the right thing. And I got a response from the New York Daily Times; they said my article received so many responses and the best news of all is that Lance and I are leaving for the Bahamas tomorrow. He has next week off so we're leaving Sunday to get the week started."

Meghan cheered, "Cali! Now that's the news I've been waiting to hear! You deserve a vacation! Have a good time and please loosen up, 'because I know you're stiff. But please give the man a little more than a kiss."

"Well gees tell me how you really feel." Cali said with a hearty laugh at her friend. "For the record you'll be very proud to know that I went shopping on my own."

Meghan hollered through the phone. "Shut up girl! You just made the baby turn."

"Seriously Meg, I bought bathing suits and sun dresses. One of the bathing suits, you're goanna love but you can't wear it until you have the baby."

"I'm sure you did great." Making herself sound sad she offered, "Well, I guess you don't need me anymore."

Cali passed her favorite color of polish to the attendant, "awe, come on now. You know I would make up something just to need you. I love you Meg! You've showed me so many things and have brought me a long way. I didn't know how to walk in heels, didn't know how to pick out a dress, and couldn't put on lipstick."

Meghan interrupted, "Now wait Cali, you still can't put that on which is why I gave you lip gloss honey."

Laughing at Meghan's silliness Cali went on to say, "Well girl, let me let them finish my nails and I also have a hair appointment later today. I'm getting some highlights in my hair."

Meghan beamed and rubbed her belly; she knew it was like to be newly in love. "Cali, this is your time. Go and be happy with Lance. Have a nice trip, as a matter of fact I know you will; he's a nice guy. I just know he's going to be my brother- in-law."

Doug wandered in behind and heard Meghan's side of the conversation. "Who's going on a vacation?"

Megan looked at her husband-to-be, "Cali and Lance, they're going to the Bahamas."

Doug gestured towards her stomach, "When you drop that mother-load we'll be going back to the Bahamas ourselves."

With a smirk, she replied, "Doug, baby, that's how we got this mother- load in the first place. So go clean those string beans please."

Doug snuck a kiss on her cheek and was glad to do as told. "Yes dear."

She returned her attention to Cali, "Cali, I love you. Call me when you get back. Oh, and don't forget to take plenty of pictures!"

After getting her toes and nails re-done she had some time to kill until her hair appointment. She decided to get something to eat. She ate light to make sure she looked good in her bathing suits. She couldn't help but imagine what this trip would be like as she munched on a salad and sipped her tea. Finished with her lunch, it was finally time to make a change with her hair. She felt she already had beautiful hair but knew the highlights would make her face look radiant.

Cali was admiring the job her stylist had just completed when Lance called her to see if she had everything she needed for their trip. She answered with a glee, "Yes, I most certainly do. And guess what else? The hospital sent me an e-mail to see if I had changed my mind about coming back and would give me until noon Monday."

Lance wanted to know; worried his plans would fall through if she chose to go back. "How do you feel about that?"

"It's nice to know they want me to stay, but I can never go back and I know they say to never say never but Lance I can't go back there." Cali lamented as she paid for her services with a hefty tip.

He agreed wholeheartedly, "Well don't; I have your back, no matter what you decide."

Cali almost started crying again but remembered she was around a salon full of people. On her walk back to her car she said, "Lance I told Meghan today I could not have asked for a better friend in her and now you; how lucky can one person be? I thank you for all the support you have shown me and one day I hope I'm able to repay you."

Lance felt all mushy inside from her sentiments, "You just did."

"How is that?" she wondered.

"By going away with me, besides don't you know; anything that bothers you, bothers me?"

"Lance, you know I use to look at you and shake my head because I just couldn't understand why you were still single, but now I know God saved you just for me."

They conversed until she'd made it home and sat comfortably on her patio sharing her feelings with the love of her life. She couldn't believe; she had a love of her life. The thought overwhelmed her.

Lance interrupted her thoughts, "I will be there to pick you up tomorrow morning at eight o'clock sharp, so get some sleep."

Saying their good nights, Cali prepared to do just that. She poured herself a glass of wine and took another long bubble bath that night. Her mind became convoluted with notions of how she knew she and Lance would finally be together. She was nervous and happy all at the same time because she had never been with a man before. In her heart, she felt if she was goanna be with one then he was definitely the right one. The thought felt a little awkward, but she trusted Lance and knew he would never do anything she didn't want to do. She blinked rapidly and figured besides if he kisses like he did before he would make her melt in his arms. Cali drifted off to sleep with dreams of special intimacy dancing through her head.

The next morning Lance was there on time as promised. When he knocked on the door Cali was looking refreshed and ready to go. Lance kissed her and asked, "Where are your bags?" She pointed towards the hallway. He asked one last time, "Do you have everything you need?"

She nodded yes.

"Do you have your passport?"

Cali's mouth opened as wide as a cannon. "I completely forgot about my passport! I'll get it! It's in my night stand." When Cali returned from getting her passport she looked at Lance and said, "Now, can you see I can't do anything without you?"

He simply smiled. She gave him the key to the door because she knew he would eventually ask for it. Cali grabbed one of the smaller suitcases and headed down the stairs. Once they made it down stairs she saw a stretch limo waiting. She turned to Lance, "Is this for us?"

"Yes my dear, nothing but the best for you."

Cali shook her head and looked at him and asked with a smile, "Just who are you?"

Kissing her on the cheek he responded with passion, "You'll soon find out."

The limo driver got out and opened the doors and then took the bags they were holding and placed them in the trunk. When they got to the airport they stopped at the airport café to get some coffee. Lance was so good at planning this trip Cali couldn't help asking him how many other women had he just whisked away on an exotic trip. Lance laughed because the tone of her voice was not one of a jealous woman, but of someone that really wanted to know.

Lance replied coolly, "You may not believe me but you're the first. Cali, you make me want to do all the things I ever wanted to but I wanted the right person to share these types of moments with and you were the one. It just amazes me that women find it so hard to believe men like romantic getaways too; especially when we know it will be stress free. And now my question to you is; why is it so hard for you to accept the things I do for you is because you deserve it and I enjoy so much doing them for you?"

Cali affirmed, "Lance, I have never even let a man get close to me, even as a teenager I never dated, but with you it feels different. You've taken time to get know me and that meant a lot. So I guess when I question why you do the things you do, I have never had anyone to compare it to, but you have set the bar very high for the next one; if there's a next one.

Lance's chest stood out territorially, "What do you mean next one? I have staked my claim on you lady." They enjoyed a moment to kiss and went about their way to board the flight. They heard the flight announcement as they finished their coffee and ran to get in line.

Chapter 15

Once they boarded and had given their tickets to the stewardess, she directed them to first class. Cali didn't want to sit by the window, but she did. When she sat down she immediately closed the shades.

Lance noticed and asked, "Are you okay?"

She answered trying to sound brave, "Yes." Afraid to mention she was actually afraid to fly. She was so excited about going away she didn't think about it until she actually boarded the plane and of course it was too late. The good thing was, in first class it was very roomy so she didn't feel like she was in an airplane. Cali grabbed one of the soft pillows they were offering and put the chair in a lounge position and laid back; she was not going to allow anything to interfere with this trip, not even a plane.

Lance snuck away and made a quick call to the realtor about the office space for Cali. After pressing end and making his way back to their seat, he grabbed a couple of Pier water bottles from the refreshment cart. He offered her a bottle of which she accepted. Cali looked at the name on the bottle. He mentioned, "This is why I like first class, Pier water." They both laugh at his joke.

They announced over the intercom they would be leaving in ten minutes. At this, Cali grabbed Lance's hand. He looked over at her, "Are you afraid to fly?"

Swallowing hard, she replied, "A little."

He held her hand tighter to give her some reassurance, "Why didn't you tell me?"

"Because this year I am facing my fears and this is one of them. To be honest I didn't think about it until we boarded the plane." Cali began to brace herself for the take-off.

Lance held her hand up to his lips and kissed it. "Well, I'll protect you." He stated as if he had to the power to keep an airplane from crashing.

Cali shuddered at the mere thought of the plane just dropping out of the sky for whatever reason. "I know you will, but can I get a double shot of jack Daniels?"

Lance did a double take, "But Cali, you don't drink jack Daniels.'

"I know but it sounds like something someone brave would drink."

Lance laughed softly and raised his hand to summon a stewardess. "A double shot of Jack Daniels for the lady please."

Cali's non-ability to handle her liquor mixed with the altitude made for an interesting flight; after a couple of bars of ninety nine bottles of beer on the wall Cali went out like a light. Lance kissed her on the forehead and covered her with the blanket.

They arrived in the Bahamas late that afternoon. Cali smiled drunkenly after noticing Lance had another limo waiting there for them. "Wow, another limo? I can get used to this." Lance had called ahead to make sure it was stocked with fruits and snacks during one of his in-flight restroom breaks because Cali had not eaten the entire plane-ride. As soon as they made themselves comfortable inside Lance opened the sun roof; he wanted Cali to smell the salt in the air, feel the awesome breeze and the beautiful warmth of the sunshine; with them having an hour ride. As they enjoyed the ocean view ride Cali noticed a beautiful white house on the beach with a white picket fence, a large wrap-around porch that appeared to wrap around the entire house.

Intrigued, Cali pointed, "Isn't that a beautiful house?"

He smiled, "Do you like that house?"

Still a bit woozy but sober enough to comprehend, she said, "Yes."

Lance kissed her on the forehead before saying, "Good, because that's where we're staying."

A gasped escaped her lips, "You've got to be kidding me."

Lance offered with a nonchalant shrug knowing he'd outdone himself with this trip. "I'm afraid not." The limo pulled down into a winding driveway towards the picturesque house. As they pulled up to the front door some of the servants came out with welcoming smiles on their faces, with their lilting accents; "Hello Dr. Trent."

Lance returned the greeting. Cali looked over to Lance, "Honey, how do these people know you?"

Lance smiled with a gleam of love and desire shining as bright as the Caribbean sunshine in his eyes. "This is my house and they work for me."

Cali was truly impressed. The property was definitely a scene from a vacation postcard. Lance led the way as they entered the house. Cali said, "This house is immaculate! How do you keep it so nice when you're not here?"

"Everyone still works here making sure that it is kept up and running." He took a hold of her hand and continued to lead her on a tour of his home away from home.

Cali continue with her questions as she admired the décor of the sitting room; the walls a soft maize with cream trim. Eclectic pieces of art and statues were strategically placed throughout the room with sheer curtains to allow as much light as possible. She ran her fingers along the mantelpiece; "Do you rent the house when you're not here?"

He'd made himself comfortable as the butler set drinks on the coffee table. "Nah, there are too many memorable things here. I don't want people going through them; this is a family house I grew up here." He watched her familiarize herself and smiled as his eyes scanned the length of her body.

"I'm sorry; I didn't know."

Lance stretched and removed his shoes. "Oh no, no need for sorry; they were good memories. This house was left to me by my grandmother. I used to come and would stay here every summer."

One of the servants brought their bags inside and asked where he wanted him to put them. Even though Cali told lance know she felt about him; the same way he did about her; he did not want to make the mistake in assuming Cali was ready to sleep with him. He'd already promised separate rooms, so he told the servant to but her bags in the largest guest room and his in the master suite.

A full framed woman with long thick hair, a beautiful broad smile, and eyes that twinkled with every breath she took seemingly waltzed into the room. In her Bahamian accent she admonished with a cluck of her tongue; "Ahh, Lance how long will I have to wait for my hug?"

Lance stood with fervor and made his way quickly to her and gave her the kind of hug that showed Cali he hadn't seen her in a while. She rocked him from side to side, held him back to get a good look at him, and then hugged him again. Throwing his arm around her shoulders, he introduced her to Cali, "Cali this is Emma. She took care of me when I was a little boy. She worked for my grandmother and when she died I just couldn't see this house without Emma. So she's continued here to make sure the house is kept up." Emma beamed with pride as she looked from Lance to Cali. "Even though she doesn't live here she comes by to check in on the place."

She pulled Cali into her arms, "You can give me a hug too. Welcome child!"

Cali laughed along with them and complimented her on the care she had shown the house.

Emma thought to herself; "Cali must be someone special because Lance has never brought any other women to this house." She was glad to see he'd finally found someone. She was so glad to see him she couldn't stop smiling and she could clearly see he was in love. Emma asked, "May I get you both something to eat or drink?"

Cali requested, "Oh, just some coffee for right now."

"I would like some too." Lance smiled up at her.

While Emma left to prepare the coffee, Cali asked Lance to show her where her room was because she wanted to take a quick shower to freshen up. Lance pulled her to her feet and into his arms. He held her for a moment before leading her up the winding staircase to her room. Cali was in awe; the guest room he took her to was bigger than her whole apartment. The walls in this room were an apricot crème with snow white trim with wicker furniture. The white sheer floor length curtains bellowed in from the afternoon breeze lifting a pleasant aroma from the bouquet of fresh cut frangipani's that were placed around the room.

Cali walked over to the curtains to realize there were double doors that opened to a small patio. She whirled around to face Lance. "You truly have a beautiful home. I'm surprised you haven't packed up all of your things and moved here for good."

Lance wrapped his arms around her waist from behind and whispered into her ear. "Thank you. I do enjoy it here when I visit. It's a great get away from everything else in the world so maybe someday we will." Cali leaned back into his embrace; her heart quivered at the word "we".

He asked, "Do you want to go to the beach or rest a little? It feels so good around this time of day."

Cali said, "No, no sleep! I don't what to lose not even one day of this beautiful sunshine."

"Okay, I will see you down stairs then." He chuckled.

She turned around to face him and kissed him lightly on the lips. "Thank you."

Kind of surprised, he asked, "For what?"

She nuzzled his neck. "For being so patient and understanding; I know most men would have stopped seeing me a long time ago. If for no other reason than they could not get to what they call second base, but you have truly shown me that you care about me and want more than just a physical relationship."

Lance stared into her eyes, "Cali, I don't just care; I love you." They planted one of those knock your shoes off kind of kisses on one another. That feeling of blood rushing in their ears, hearts pounding, and overwhelming passion came over them. They both knew this would be a week to remember. It took a moment to keep from taking things too far; with all the strength they had; they departed. Cali took a moment to gather her emotions; she stood on the patio for a few moments to appreciate her surroundings. Lance left to take a very cold shower.

*****

Feeling renewed from her shower she sprayed some new perfume she'd purchased. She didn't care it would be washed off once they made it to the beach. She wanted lance to be mesmerized by her fragrance. Before making her way downstairs, she paused in front of the mirror and modeled one of her one piece bathing suits she bought; she'd even lucked up and found the skirt to match; she was very proud of herself because she finally didn't have to rely on Meghan to do it for her. Even though she liked her to do it, she had to face the fact that Meghan would be having her own family to take care of. Admiring herself; she turned and posed like a pin-up, she thought further, besides they weren't kids anymore. Suddenly, it dawned on her how far she'd come from not understanding her own sexuality to feeling like she was falling in love with a wonderful man her first time out. Cali had come to terms with her feelings that before this trip was over she would give herself to Lance completely.

Chapter 16

Cali heard a knock on the door; even though she was wearing a bathing suit she still grabbed a robe and opened the door. It was Emma bringing her coffee. Cali thanked her, "You didn't have to bring this up; I could've gotten it when I came down."

Emma shushed her, "I don't mind at all. And there's more down stairs if you find you want another cup."

She thanked her again. Before leaving, Emma gave Cali a thoughtful look before speaking her mind. "I've never seen Lance so happy."

Cali blushed. "Well he keeps me pretty happy too. Sometimes I think I'm dreaming and if I am I don't want anyone to wake me up."

Emma patted her arm, "That's sweet to hear. Ms. Cali if you need anything while you're here, just let me know."

"Okay Ms. Emma." Emma left Cali alone to finish dressing for the beach.

After Lance had taken his shower and changed into his beach attire he had Emma pack them a picnic basket for the beach along with two bottles of chilled wine from the wine cellar. Cali came down the steps feeling fancy and free; she was glowing with love and she didn't care who noticed. She'd never been so happy in her life. She'd only been on the island for a few hours and already the Bahamas was doing her some good. She was away from everything that made her sad and with a man that adored her and would do anything to please her. The only thing she missed about home was her best friend Meghan.

Lance reached for her hand as she came down the stairs. As they headed out of the front door Emma stopped them; "Would you like me to fix dinner for you?"

"Now Emma, you've done enough. No we'll find somewhere to eat if we get hungry. You should go home and enjoy the rest of your evening. I will need you tomorrow morning to prepare breakfast though. You okay with that?" Giving her another big hug and kiss on the cheek she pushed him back towards the door and they left for the beach.

Lance led the way to the four car garage where he had Cali choose which car they would be driving; even though the beach was just yards from his house he wanted to take her to a special part of the beach where it was very secluded and they could watch the sun set. Each new thing she learned about Lance amazed Cali all the more; for one, he was connoisseur of fine things. There were four vehicles to choose from; a jet black luxury Jaguar that gleamed as if it was still on the show room floor to a four wheel Jeep.

He urged her once again to pick what she wanted to ride in. She didn't think twice; "The jeep will be cool. I want to feel the wind in my face."

Now Lance wasn't testing her but was shocked at her choice. He thought most women would have picked the Jaguar or Corvette or even the convertible Mercedes, but she chose the Jeep. He repeated it to himself again, "Wow, she chose the plain little jeep." His curiosity peaked as to why out of all of those cars did she choose the jeep. "Are you sure you want us to drive the jeep?"

She replied, "Of course. I think the jeep can move around better in the sand than those luxury cars here. They look so pretty I wouldn't want them to get dirty from the sand."

Lance shook his head and smiled. "Alright then, the jeep it is." He went over to his key keeper and got the keys for the jeep, some pillows, blankets and wood chips to make a fire. He kept those types of things in the garage for moments like this and emergency. As they bumped their way down to the beach Lance admitted his thoughts to

Cali, "You know, most women would have likely chosen one of the other cars."

Laughing because she'd figured as much, she brushed a strand of hair behind her ear; "That is what I have been told for most of my life; that I do most things different from most women. I wonder if that's good or bad."

Glancing at her, Lance said, "I find it to be good. You are uncomplicated and easy to please. One of the reasons I love you." Lance took Cali's hand and kissed it.

It was about a fifteen minute drive; they arrived at what Lance called his private beach. Cali knew why he wanted to bring her there; it was absolutely breath taking. When she stepped out of the jeep the tranquility nearly swept her off of her feet. The sky looked so close, she wanted to reach out and touch it. Her feet sank in the soft warm sand which only enhanced her pedicured feet. And the beautiful teal blue water beckoned her to come in. Lance called out to Cali to show her where they would be setting up. He'd watched her walking towards the water as if in a trance. Lance ran to join her. They left everything sitting in the jeep and enjoyed the warm tropical water.

Lance and Cali swam out to fully enjoy the depths of the water. They kissed and held each other as their bodies entwined; realizing they were approaching the buoys, Lance suggested they swim back to shore. He playfully chased Cali back to shore and they collapsed onto the wet sands exhausted; stomachs cramped with laughter.

"Woo, I didn't realize we swam out that far." She began brushing sand off of her legs, holding her head back to bask in the waning sunlight.

Lance explained, "That's why I suggested we return."

He reached to move hair out of her face as she began to speak, "I've never been to the beach."

"You could have fooled me; the way you swam out there."

Cali laughed and playfully shoved him. "I learned how to swim in school."

Lance wondered, "Didn't your mother or father take you to the beach?"

Sucking her teeth with a slight attitude she replied, "They never took me anywhere."

Lance could see the hurt in Cali's eyes and watched her as she started to zone out into deep thought. He scooted closer, "I'll take you everywhere you want to go."

Those simple words touched her heart in ways she couldn't explain. She turned her head towards Lance's chest and began to cry. Lance had never seen Cali cry and that kind of frightened him. She'd always come across so strong. Lance tried to console her, "Don't cry. This was supposed to be a good time. Do you want to leave?"

She sniffed and wiped her face, "No, I'm sorry; I was just thinking about the horrible time I had as a child and teen. That's why I talk about Meghan so much; she's helped me get through some of my worst times. She was the only one I could talk to."

Lance wanted to know; "You were so young; why weren't your parents there for you?"

Preparing to divulge her odd childhood she admitted, "They were part of the problem. When I was about five, my dad re-enlisted in the military. By the time I was about seven he had completely moved out. He never said why and neither did my mother; she just kept saying it's something they couldn't talk about. My dad never attended my high school graduation, not even when I graduated from college."

Lance was a taken back; "Cali, if you had not told me I would not have known that you went through anything like this. You always conduct yourself like you haven't a care in the world."

As Cali continued to wipe tears from her eyes she said, "I was really crying because I'm happy for the first time in my life and I can say I'm truly happy."

Lance gave her a little shake, "Now see there, there you go."

Cali looked confused at what lance was saying, "See what?"

"See; now you're doing something like most women." He couldn't help but to laugh at her. She moved to hit him but he ran towards the jeep and she ran after him laughing as well. They set up a make-shift cabana just in case it got windy and placed a blanket in front of the cabana. Lastly, they grabbed the picnic basket and the wine from the jeep. Lance poured them both a glass of wine and turned on the portable radio. This time he didn't have to ask Cali to dance; she pulled him up. She had been practicing alone in front of her mirror and had actually gotten pretty good. They laughed, danced and swam some more until the sun began its descent below the horizon. It turned out to be a great day.

Packing up to head home; Cali confirmed in her heart she was going to finally give herself to Lance. She no longer wanted to deny herself the pleasures of being with someone she cared about; she no longer wanted to be alone. She thought of how Meghan has found love and about to start a family. Then she thought of how she was still finding herself sexually; while this wonderful man who loves her and does anything for her. No, she could not bear to lose Lance and she felt it was no longer fair to him to make him wait and more importantly she was ready.

When they pulled up to Lance's house Emma was just leaving; she told them she'd cooked dinner anyway and that she'd be back in the morning to still cook them breakfast. After giving a round of hugs and kisses to each of them she went about her way. Even though Cali liked Emma as soon as they had met; she was glad she'd left; it would be hard enough to be with Lance for the first time and even harder with someone else other than Lance being in the house. Cali got turned around and headed back to the jeep for the unopened bottle of wine they'd left inside of the picnic basket. Upon entering the house she walked up to Lance and kissed him. He was happily shocked to see her initiate a kiss from him, but Lance had no idea what type of initiation was next; he allowed her to make all of the moves. She put her tongue in his mouth and Lance nearly lost his balance from the sensations she evoked in him; she sent sparks to personal places in his body.

She took his hand and led him up the stairs. For the first time Lance was afraid; she'd totally caught him off guard. But he wasn't going to let fear keep him from going with the flow of wherever she was taking him; he'd waited for her too long and may never get the chance to be with her again. Cali pushed the door of the guest room open. Lance followed her inside and shut the door behind him. The passion each felt electrified the room. The lust that had been restrained burst forth suddenly; losing all control; they kissed from the door and eventually made their way to the bed. Since they were wearing swimming clothes they didn't have much material to remove. Lance watched as she removed her bathing suit. He felt like he was looking at a gift being unwrapped. Her firm breasts and well-toned body captivated him. Cali was equally mesmerized by Lance's tan colored skin and the muscles she'd had the pleasure of feeling when they hugged but now felt even more elated to see they were real.

They're bodies twisted and turned with each other as they explored each other; learning likes and dislikes; taking each moment to tempt, nibble, taste. Cali finally spread her legs and allowed Lance to enter her. Once he penetrated the very part she held so sacred Lance went wild inside; to finally have his beloved Cali. Each stroke felt like a piece of heaven to him; Cali was equally delighted to feel him inside of her body. They made love what seemed like for hours; they could no longer hold themselves; they climaxed again, again, and again. Screams of ecstasy could be heard throughout the house. Lance had never been with a woman who made love to every part of his body and allowed him to make love to every part of hers. He felt in his heart at that very moment there could never be anyone other than Cali; she already had his mind and now she owned his body. Cali had had no other lovers other than Lance, but she knew she would never want another herself.

They lay in bed as their bodies still jerked from the after effects of their love making. Cali turned her back to take in the feeling she never thought she would be feeling. It overwhelmed her to the point of wanting to give in to her emotions again and just cry, but instead she basked in the afterglow of their love. Lance kissed her back, neck and kissed his way to her buttocks. He began to spread her buttocks; when he received no resistance, Cali pushed herself towards him so he could gain full access to her. He penetrated her body once again; Cali went wild. They climaxed again and fell asleep in each other's arms.

When Lance awoke, he decided to call Emma letting her know he wouldn't need her for the rest of the week, but he wanted to see her before he left. He smiled as she proclaimed she understood he wanted time alone with the new love of his life. She teased him before hanging up. He climbed back into bed with Cali. He wanted to wake her up to love; he planted kisses along the skin of her neck that was exposed, down to her shoulder, around to her breasts. She groaned from the butterflies stirring deep within her belly. Her eyes fluttered open; at first she thought she was dreaming but quickly realized what Lance was up to. Fully awake, they started kissing and made love throughout the rest of the early morning. Neither understood the uncontrollable passion they felt for each other and did nothing to resist it.

Chapter 17

Later that morning Lance got up to take a shower; he noticed Cali was still a sleep. He kissed her gently so as not to disturb her rest and went down stairs to surprise her with breakfast. What Cali didn't know was that Lance was an awesome cook. He'd never gotten the chance to cook for her so he was determined to show off his culinary skills. He'd watched and sometimes helped his grandmother and Emma around the kitchen.

The rich aroma of coffee traveled up the stairs and made its way to Cali's nose. It woke her up; she turned over and snuggled further underneath the covers remembering the sessions of love she'd just experienced. Finally, she stumbled into the bathroom and ran herself a hot bath; her body was sore. She gently emerged her body into the hot bubbled water and settled back. Cali continued to reminisce about her and Lance finally being together the night before. Just the day before it was still unclear who she was; now she felt like a real woman in love with a man. Fate had finally stepped in and she was glad about it.

She heard a soft knock on the door. "Come in." she called out; knowing it was Lance. He had a cup of coffee for her. As she sat up in the water, she said with appreciation; "Just what the doctor ordered."

He offered, "I made you breakfast too."

She asked, "Don't tell me you cook too?" Then remembered the dinner he'd wanted to cook for her.

He nodded his head, "Yep."

She heard her stomach rumble with hunger. "What did you cook?"

"Hot cakes; I'll fix your eggs when you come down, so don't rush, enjoy your bath."

He left Cali to enjoy her bath and went to check his e-mail. There was one from the realtor to look at the offices he'd found for Cali. Lance e-mailed him back on the one he thought Cali would like based on her wish list. Lance remembered her favorite colors were peach and ivory, so he instructed him to have the designer to decorate using those colors. He reiterated in his reply he wanted it finished by the time they returned. He stood up from his desk with satisfaction settling around his shoulders as he felt that day would be the day he would ask Cali to marry him. The more he thought about how he would ask the more he broke out into a sweat. He grew nervous and felt like a school boy. He continued to wonder as he waited on her to finish her bath; how was he going to propose? Was the ring big enough?

Cali finished her bath, dressed, and went down stairs to join Lance for breakfast. He pulled out her chair and asked her, "How would you like your eggs?"

"Lightly scrambled is fine." She answered with a hint of flirtation.

He moved towards the stove, "Coming right up my dear." It was kind of funny for Cali to see him cooking and setting the table because at work he was so serious and in charge, but she loved both sides of him.

*****

After eating breakfast Lance offered, "Would you like to go for a walk on the beach?"

She jumped from her seat excitedly and moved to go upstairs and get ready. Lance glanced up as she descended the stairs and smiled admiringly at what she was wearing. "You look so beautiful to me, but then again you could wear a chicken suit and still be beautiful."

Cali laughed at his comment feeling more womanly than she'd ever felt. Her outfit was simple, pair of turquoise palazzo pants with a black camisole and matching black sandals; she didn't feel comfortable or awkward in any way; besides they were going just one hundred feet from Lance's home. Before heading out; she took her hair out of the pony tail and shook it out her chestnut brown hair cascaded in layers around her shoulders.

Lance held Cali's hands and thought to himself, "We are finally a couple."

The skyline was alive with purple, pink, yellow, and orange as the sun made its appearance for the day. The shoreline was peaceful as the tide rushed towards them. There were a couple of wooden lounge chairs that belonged to Lance's grandmother in good condition they came upon as they made their way down to the beach. Cali took a seat in one of the chairs; she was glad Lance had asked her to come out for a walk; she could us a tan right about now. Lounging back in the chair she relaxed her mind and body and caught a little sun. In the meantime Lance murmured to himself as to how he was going to propose to Cali. She tried to look over at him with the sun in her face; "Are you okay? Come sit with me." When he did, she sat up and asked him again, "Are you alright? Is it something I've done?"

Lance found his voice and finally looked back at her, "No, no sweetheart; you did nothing wrong. That's the problem Cali; you have been doing everything right." Cali frowned in confusion with worry beginning to grip her insides. Lance pulled the ring box from his pocket and kneeled down next to her in the sand. Taking a deep breath, he asked, "Cali, would you marry me?"

Cali was in total shock as she looked at Lance to see if he was perhaps kidding with her, but she knew he wasn't the kind of person to say something like marriage and not mean it. The sparkle of the diamond drew her eyes to ring he held; that beautiful exquisite ring.

Lance was looking like a lost puppy the longer it took her to respond; what seemed like an hour was only minute. He still had not heard yes; he began to fear she would not say yes and that he was rushing her with everything that happened last night. Regret replaced the nervousness he'd just felt as the scene in his head was totally different from what was actually happening. "Sorry, I'm rushing you aren't I?"

Cali finally spoke, "No, you're not rushing me at all, but are you sure you what to marry me Lance?" she asked; trying to give him a way out while he had the chance. Lance remained on his knees as he made his pitch to convince her to say yes; "Cali, look at me; I bought this ring before we left home. I had plans on asking you to marry me when we got here. Trust me; it had nothing to do with last night. Last night only confirmed how I feel about you. Cali you asked me was I sure I wanted to marry you; woman, I have never been so sure of anything in my life. I think about you every day. I love being around you and I worry about you when I'm not. You're unreadable, which I love and that keeps my heart with you. Your kisses are unbelievable and your love making drove me crazy. I want to come home to you and only you Cali."

His speech stirred emotions within and her water works turned on full time; Cali shook her head up and down; "Yes, Lance, I will marry you!"

Lance placed the engagement ring on Cali's finger; they shared a passionate kiss as the sun shown round and full over the horizon. Lance promised her he would always take care of her and she would never want for anything. Cali paused, "Lance, may I ask you a question? You gave me three destinations to choose; what if I had said Hawaii? Do you own a house there too?"

Lance gave a small laugh, "No, but I do own a hotel there. And I own a resort in aspen."

Cali's curiosity increased at his answer. "Lance, I asked you before, who were you when we left home and you said I would find out; so who is my future husband?"

Lance got up from the ground, settled into the chair next to hers, and wiped his knees as he began to explain. "My family was rich Cali." He stated simply. "To be even more honest, very rich; my grandfather owned two oil wells and when he died it went to my father. When he passed away I was too young to inherit anything, but when my grandmother passed everything was willed to me. Cali, I'm a billionaire; being a doctor is just what I enjoy doing. Can you live with that?"

Cali's mouth hung open from hearing his confession. "Oh my God, Lance! You act like any other normal person.

Lance laughed. "I am. And I'm proud to be a doctor. That's something I earned, no one gave that to me."

Cali reached over to touch his arm. "That's not what I mean. I'm sorry, it's just that; you don't have a body guard like most billionaires would have. Don't you think you should have one?"

Lance was truly tickled by her assumption. He leaned comfortably in the chair. "Cali, there are a lot of millionaires walking around among us and they do not have a body guard."

Cali stared out over the blue-green water trying to wrap her head around this latest revelation. "Yeah, I guess that would be a little creepy too; people walking around with another person shadowing them as if they were the president or some diplomat, but Lance you're a billionaire; that's a tad bit different from being a millionaire don't ya' think?"

Lance shrugged, "I guess. But think about it; I'm a doctor; how crazy would it look for me to have a body guard at the hospital. Besides, I can't have one in the patient's room while I'm examining them, now could I? I like to be known as a doctor not a billionaire; to me being a doctor comes first. So now you know when we get married you'll be a billionaire too."

"Whoa now, you're moving too fast. I don't know if I can give up McDonald's or Burger King." She laughed along with him. Lance put his hands on his chin, "Yeah that would be hard. I don't want to ask too much of you." Their laughter danced away over the tides as they further enjoyed their surroundings and each other.

Lance snapped his fingers and sat forward as he remembered to mention, "Hey! There's a beach bonfire party tonight I want to take you to; you're going to have such a great time! There will be dancers and there's usually someone cooking over an open fire; roasting a pig and some other meats, oh, and plenty of fireworks! It usually lasts through the night. Think you can hang that long?" He chided with a sly smile.

Cali had never experienced a beach bonfire party before and was excited at just the thought. She stood up and did her goofy happy dance; usually reserved for just she and Meghan; but she felt so free with Lance she didn't care. Lance stood and joined in the happy dance which surprised Cali; they toppled into one another and fell in the sand in fits of more laughter. Love was in the air all around them and there was nothing anyone could do about it. She was ready to go back to the house for some rest for the night's festivities.

Chapter 18

The housekeeper was just finishing up with washing their breakfast dishes and making their beds when Cali and Lance arrived back to the house. They asked Lance if he needed anything before leaving; he nodded no. But then told Marc, the grounds keeper to bring around the Mercedes; it was a cute little red convertible. Recalling the openness of her smile from riding in the jeep, he knew Cali would appreciate to feel the breeze of the beach on this beautiful day when they went out to party.

Later that evening after a nice long rest Cali got ready for the beach bonfire party; she chose to wear the white haltered sun dress that flowed like the petals of a flower with every move she made. She pinned her hair up and put on a pair of sea shell earrings she purchased from the airport gift shop. A pair of low wedge heeled sandals completed the look she was going for. Cali twirled around in front of the mirror, her new ritual; and was highly pleased she was getting better with dressing herself. She remembered, Meghan said she didn't need much make up; just a little eyeliner and lip gloss; she was ready to go. Just as she was about to turn the door handle to meet Lance downstairs, she glanced down at her beautiful ring. Tears threatened to fall once again as she thought back to his loving proposal. She couldn't wait to fill Meghan in on all of the details, especially the look he had on his face when he thought she was about to say no.

This date was no different than any other; Cali and Lance once again found themselves having the same color scheme. Lance looked like a GQ model with his beige leisure suit and brown dress sandals. Lance walked out of the kitchen just as Cali seemingly floated into the living room; seeing she was ready, he grabbed the keys, but then remembered a shawl his grandmother used to wear he thought was so beautiful. He put it in the car just in case Cali got cold. Lance, ever the gentleman, opened the car door for his bride to be, shut it gingerly, and ran around to the driver's side.

When they arrived, the bonfire party was in full swing; people were everywhere just having a good time. They were dancing, drinking, and eating. The tide was out; the moon full and the music contagious. The reggae band consisted of a steel drum player who laid the foundation for the singer who crooned about the freedom of love and dancing the night away. His two back ground singers carried the melody along with the bass guitar player who strummed the strings as if his life depended on it. They heard the music from the highway giving Cali that anxious feeling that something exciting was about to happen. It took a few minutes to find a parking space. Lance could tell Cali was ready to mingle and join in the fun.

The beat called to them as they held hands and meandered through the crowd. They joined the dancing crowd and allowed the beat of the music to carry them away. In a trance, Cali danced with her eyes closed and shook her hips to the music. She opened her eyes and noticed her handsome fiancé' was smiling at her; she smiled back, leaning in to speak close to his ear, "This is wonderful! I can't believe some people call this place home." She continued swaying as she yelled over the sounds of the music. Lance suddenly grabbed her hands and turned her to the beat. A slight dip, he held his hand steady on her back and pulled her firmly into his embrace. He whispered coarsely, "Marry me right now."

Cali was bewildered and wanted to be sure she'd heard him correctly, "What did you say?"

"Marry me; here in the Bahamas." He pleaded.

Cali arched an eyebrow, "Here; right now? But I would like to have Meghan here." She whined.

Lance reasoned, "Honey, Meghan is getting married herself soon and once we get home we can just have another celebration with family and friends. I want you to go home as my wife."

Cali thought aloud, "Well, when I go home I will be getting ready for Meghan's wedding. And I don't want her to turn right around and get ready for another wedding; I want her to fully enjoy hers."

Lance kissed her, "So, does that mean we can get married tonight and tell them later?"

For some reason Cali felt everything was working out right between her and Lance; she trusted him with her life. With no further thought she threw caution to the wind and yelled, "Let's do it!"

He lifted her off her feet and spun around, "Do you mean it?"

"Yes! I know Meghan would be happy for me."

Lance look into Cali eyes; "I will never make you regret marrying me." He reiterated his earlier sentiment. "You will never want for anything as long as you live."

Cali admired him wanting to do all of this for her but still stated, "Lance don't you have a pre-nuptial agreement or something for me to sign?"

Lance shook his head, "Nope, no prenup. A billion dollars; how much can one person want? I don't have anyone but you Cali and I trust you with my life."

Hearing those words, she reassured him. "I would never hurt you. I don't have money like you but I have enough to take care of myself so I need you understand I am not marrying you for your money, but because I love you, the man; Lance." She confirmed with a poke of her finger into his chest.

*****

They left the bonfire party and went to find a priest on the island to marry them. He drove them to town where he'd remembered seeing a chapel that offered weddings twenty-four hours a day. He figured whoever came up with the idea for it must've seen many people searching for a way to marry on a whim. The little white chapel sat on the corner of the town square. A couple was coming out wearing smiles and headed in the direction of the bar down the street. The mood was definitely festive as vacationers milled about like ants. Both hoped they wouldn't have long to wait as they made their way to the entrance. Cali paused on the front step and looked up at the blinking sign that read, "Welcome to Light of Love Chapel – Weddings 24-7". Lance looked back hoping she wasn't changing her mind. She stepped up to stand toe to toe with him; stared into his eyes and kissed him with the passion she was feeling. "I love you Dr. Lance Roberts, Replying" I love too Dr. Cali Evans.

The chapel attendant welcomed them with a gracious smile and then asked them to fill out the necessary papers to make their marriage legally binding, as they both signed the paper Cali kidded Lance okay here's your chance to back out. Lance just smile and said never, both of my eyes are wide open Cali, at that moment Cali really realized that her life was about to change forever and she was also stepping in with eyes wide open. The signing was finished the fees were paid now it was time for a wedding. The attendant placed the islands flower in Cali's hair. She then handed her freshly picked flowers as her bouquet and motion them to follow her. The minister, a soft spoken gentleman, led them outside; as they stood in the sand, a beautiful mural of a multicolor sunset with still blue waters was used as a back drop; a picture that even Van Gogh could not have captured. After the minister pronounced them man and wife, Cali and Lance just stood in a daze; they were married. The minister broke the silence with a tender announcement; smiling as he said, "You may kiss your bride." Lance leaned in and kissed Cali; and just as the open air their spirits flew free; Cali was now Mrs. Lance Roberts.

When they got home Lance carried Cali over the threshold; laughing in surprise, she'd forgotten about that part. But something else she noticed was this was the second time that night he'd picked her up; she did not know he was so strong. Heading up the staircase, Lance nudged Cali from behind toward the master bedroom; "This is our room now." He nibbled her neck and laid her on the bed and slowly took off her clothes. He smiled down into her face knowing this time he was making love to his wife and she was making love to her husband. As he parted her legs she moaned just from his touch; that excited him to no end and he couldn't wait to be inside her again. The thrill of his penetration of what was now his gave his love making a new meaning; this was his wife. She lifted her legs and wrapped them around his waist taking a deep breath allowing him a deeper entry. They bucked wildly enjoying every ounce of their climax; one after another until they lay spent. Sweet confusion engulfed them; they could not understand their uncontrollable sexual attraction they had; they just accepted the fact their feelings for each other ran that deep.

They slept until late the next morning. Lance kissed Cali awake, "Good morning Mrs. Roberts."

Cali stretched and yawned, "Good morning Mr. Roberts."

They got up to take a shower together; she washed him and he washed her. Cali was busied herself with applying her favorite after bath oil as Lance went downstairs to the kitchen. He returned with a bottle of champagne and orange juice for mimosas, fresh strawberries, and wheat toast.

Cali was just finishing up drying her hair as Lance sat the tray down, "I didn't make us anything to eat but toast."

Cali replied after taking a sip of her mimosa, "I'm not really hungry. This toast and juice is fine to take the edge off."

Lance found he just couldn't keep his hands to himself; he walked over to her and grabbed her hand that held the ponytail holder she was about to put in her hair. "Leave it down. I like it that way." He smiled and kissed her on the neck.

She teased him. "You better stop before you start something you can't finish."

He didn't say a word as he gave them both a reason a take another shower.

*****

Lying in bed; tangled in the sheets, Lance suggested, "Do you feel like going for a swim?"

Even though she felt a bit worn out from all of their lovemaking, Cali still agreed. "Yes let me get my bathing suit."

"No need." He grunted as he hopped up out of bed, grabbed her hand, and continued. "Put this robe on. We don't have to go all the way to the beach; we can go to the pool."

Cali looked at him incredulously, "How are we to going to swim without our suits?"

He grinned wickedly; "We can skinny dip."

With a gasp; "Are you crazy? The grounds men will see us."

"No they won't." He encouraged further. "I gave everyone today off yesterday. It's just the two of us." He stated with a kiss after each word at the bottom of the stairs.

Cali released the rest of her inhibitions and allowed the robe to slide down the length of her body. She closed her eyes and stood still to feel the warmth of the sun touch every single part of her naked body. A few moments passed before she lowered herself into the pool and enjoyed the water. Lance joined her after watching disrobe; he was ready to make love to her again but restrained himself. Instead, they swam playful; lazy laps across the pool. After about seven laps she got out and meandered towards Jacuzzi. She stretched her arms above her head with a flourish. "Lance, I love it here. I don't want to go home."

He joined her in the Jacuzzi; the warm water rising to his chest. "Well, my dear, if that's what you want; we don't have to, but I would have to transfer my license here."

Cali gave him a thoughtful look. "I wouldn't want you to give up your practice and besides I have Meghan's wedding to go to."

"Well, there's always after Meghan's wedding. Nothing has to be decided right away."

A kinky idea made her warm and tingly inside. She straddled him as she forgot all about her sore muscles. "You're right about that my love. Nothing has to be decided right away. All that matters right now is the here and now."

Chapter 19

The remainder of the week went by in a flurry as they savored each other's company while letting it soak in they were now husband and wife. Lance got a call from his realtor to review some pictures on-line and to approve the finished design of Cali's office. He hurried to his office while Cali was at the farmer's market and logged on to his computer. It was absolutely stunning Lance knew Cali would love it the moment she stepped through the doors. He couldn't wait for them to see it in person. He sent the realtor a reply telling them great job and reminded them to make sure her name was on the office door. After scanning the pictures of each area one more time he made a mental note to give them a bonus for the job well done. Lance sent a second message asking his realtor to look for some houses for him and Cali to look at when they made it back. He rushed to close out of the pictures and email as he heard her pull into the drive and shut the door. He jogged to the front door to greet her and help put away the fruits and vegetables.

Lance wanted to surprise Cali with a boat ride for later that day. He'd recalled her mentioning she'd never been fishing on actual fishing boat before, so he wanted her to see she was in for a real treat. He thought of a small barrier island to venture to. He knew of one that had some good catching. The late afternoon sun wasn't as brutal as expected as they floated above the white-capped waves and caught all types of fish. He told their fishing guide to take them back to the main island where they could share the fish they caught with everyone; they ended up catching everything from fish to lobster. Cali lounged nearby as she watched Lance and their fishing guide build a fire in ground pit they roasted the seafood in. She was truly intrigued as she'd never seen anything like it and there were several fruits of the island they delighted in for dessert. Lance opened a fresh coconut they shared a drink straight from it.

As the sun began to set; a crowd gathered with music, more food, and drinks; her new favorite, the Bahamas Mama was in abundance. Cali slurped down two before the sun had completely set and once again a flower was placed in her hair. Cali was good and tipsy but was still able to string her words together quite eloquently; "There is so much beauty here. I'll never forget our time here. If we come back in the fall; I want to come back permanently." Lance smiled into his wife's flushed face and kissed her on the nose. While the food cooked, Lance and Cali took a walk further up the beach to see different vendors set up to sell an eclectic array of hand-made items. Cali used this as a good time to pick up gifts to take back with her. Right away a wooden carving of a man and woman's hand joined together caught Cali's eye; the writing read "as one". She immediately thought that would be a wonderful gift for Meghan and Doug's wedding. She also bought her mother a gift; a string of fresh water pearls with matching earrings and a sea shell bracelet.

On their walk back towards the open pit to eat, a girl with big bright eyes and a cocoa complexion bounced up from her seat with freshly braided hair. The older woman smiled and waved with her comb for Cali to come and sit. It took about twenty minutes as her fingers moved with a speed and expertise she'd never witnessed; she gazed with appreciation at herself in the hand held mirror at the Bo Derek like braids with sea shells on the end.

They returned just in time to indulge in the hot steamy seafood. To burn off the food they'd stuffed themselves with they took off their shoes to play a round of volleyball. Lance was shocked at how fast and strong Cali was with hitting the ball; her serve were unbelievable. After the volleyball game a group of people began a good old fashioned foot race; that was right up Cali's alley. Lance had no idea she was so athletic. He stood in awe as he watched her finish her race coming in a close second. She felt really out of shape because she had not raced since her school days; but refreshed none the less. Lance was so impressed with his wife's skills; "Hey, if we ever run together I hope I can keep up."

She smiled, "You don't have to worry about keeping up; I'll run slower."

"Gee, thanks." He tickled her to the ground; their laughter rang out across the beach, mixed with the other sounds of life being enjoyed.

*****

The day had been a long and eventful one for the newlyweds, but their wonderful trip was nearing an end. Cali had seen in seven days what she had not seen in her 26years, Lance had no idea how much that meant to her no word could express. She knew if nothing else good happened in her life she had these seven days to remember. Lance called Emma as soon as they walked in the house to remind her he was leaving in the morning and that he could leave without seeing her. Cali went upstairs to begin packing her bags. The next morning after breakfast; they met with Emma in the kitchen.

"Cali and I got married Emma." He announced proudly.

Tears of joy sprang from her eyes. She knew his mother and grandmother would be so happy for him to have found true happiness. Then, she stopped short of her rejoicing; "Lance? Does she really know who you are?"

He placed a hand on her shoulder reassuringly, "Yes I told her everything."

Emma wiped her tears and hugged him; "Well I am so happy for you! I know you love each other; I saw it when I first saw you two together. Where is the newest member of our family anyway?"

Cali waltzed in on cloud nine. "I'm right here Ms. Emma. How are you doing this beautiful morning?"

"Woo, chile not as well as you with that glow you have going on." Her accent got thicker by the second. "You look like you've already made me some God children."

Cali's face turned a deeper red. "I don't think so; not so soon." She hurriedly changed the subject. "It was wonderful meeting you and thank you so much for welcoming me with open arms."

Lance kissed Emma on the cheek. "We'll see you when we come back in the fall. We have to head to the airport for our flight." he handed her a hefty envelope.

One of his butlers carried their bags down to the waiting limo; he took a few moments to say goodbye to his staff. He did not need to pay anyone as it was all handled by his accountant, but he did enjoy giving extra when it was due. When they drove off Cali looked back at the house and she had a funny feeling she would never see that house again. She didn't know why she felt that way. Lance detected Cali's face change from happy to sad. He asked with concern, "What's wrong honey?"

She tried to sound cheerful with her response, "Oh, nothing." She shrugged and held his hand.

*****

Emma watched her dear sweet Lance drive off, no longer the little boy who'd wanted hugs every time he blazed into a room to fill it with his presence and high energy; and smiled as she opened the manila envelope he'd given her; one of the envelopes inside was addressed to the staffing crew and one other was addressed to Emma. When she opened the envelope for the staffing crew, she saw they were all given a five thousand dollar bonus. Emma could not believe it; but then again she could; she knew Lance was very caring but this; this would definitely help the families of the staff members. She called each staffer one by one to give them their great news and just to see their faces made her heart so very glad; some of them cried.

Emma was no longer a housekeeper but more of an overseer making sure everything was done and done to the specifications she was used to seeing; she did clean years ago but Lance's grandmother told her to retire not long before she died, but to just relax and oversee things. And that's what she did, however, on occasions she would help out if things got overwhelming or just giving someone a break because they needed to do something for their family. Everyone was made happy that day. Emma never looked in the envelope Lance gave her; she just assumed it was a five thousand dollar bonus like everyone else, at least she had hoped.

Emma helped the ladies get the house back in order because Lance would not be back for several months. After she had finished helping with the cleaning, Emma couldn't stand it any longer; she took the envelope from her apron pocket. As she opened it, she found a letter was inside. She unfolded it tenderly; in it, Lance told her he loved her like family; she was family to him and wanted her to know how much he appreciated her hard work. He went on to write how he could not have trusted anyone but her to take care of the house as his grandmother would have. He told her again he loved her and hoped she will be around for his children. Lastly, to view this simply as a token from him and his grandmother's heart. Emma looked at the check thinking to see five thousand dollars; she blinked a few more times to make sure she was seeing correctly. Still unsure, she reached into her other apron pocket for her reading glasses; it was a check in the amount of five million dollars. Emma kept staring at the hand written amount; she had never seen so many zeroes. Her knees felt weak to the point she had to sit down from the total shock; happy that someone she's worked with for thirty years thought enough of her to set her up for life. She was already paid very well for just looking out for the place but this; she could never have imagined. Emma dialed Lance's cell number to thank him. He shrugged as if she could see him, "No Emma thank you."

He enjoyed giving and planned to continue to give freely until he took his last breath.

*****

When they boarded the plane this time, Cali did not need anything to keep her calm. If that wonderful week didn't do it; nothing would. Lance noticed again something was troubling her but he didn't want to keep asking her; he knew she would tell him when she was ready.   Getting comfortable in their seats, he asked her; "Do you want anything?"

Cali smiled over at him, "No, honey I'm fine. I couldn't be better."

Lance settled back in his seat and adjusted the pillow behind his head as he began to explain part of his surprise. "I want to let you know I had my realtor look for about five houses for us to look at when we back in and settled."

Her heart swelled and felt it would burst from her chest, but reservations still shut down her excitement. "We're buying a house?"

He kissed the palm of her hand; "Well, your apartment is definitely too small for the both of us so I thought we could move into a house we both want."

Cali offered, "Could we stay at your place for now? I want this Jena's investigation to be over and then we can plan where we want to live, can't we?"

Lance took Cali's hands and turned to face her; "Whatever you want is fine with me."

"Thanks babe." Cali laid her head on his shoulder. Lance now knew why Cali expressed several times in the Bahamas she didn't want to go home because he had seen the spirit drain out of her since they boarded the plane; a heaviness hung about her he couldn't put his finger on. But he hoped a look at her new office would perk her up. Just as when they left, when the plane landed a limo was there waiting to take them from the airport. Lance gave the limo driver the address to Cali's new office; she looking with questioning eyes at Lance who didn't say a word; just pretended she wasn't staring a hole into the side of his face; Cali knew they were going in the wrong direction but he refused to look at her or answer any of her questions of why they were headed into town.

The last time Cali asked, "Lance, where are we going?"

He kissed her until she was breathless; "It's a surprise."

Cali's eyes stretched. "I don't know if I can take any more surprises."

"Well my dear." He said. "I think you're going to love this particular surprise."

The limo pulled next to the curb; Lance stepped out first and then held his hand out to assist Cali out of the car. They stood outside of a high-rise building where a grandfatherly looking doorman tipped his hat, smiled graciously, and waved them into the entrance of an immaculately decorated lobby. The gold and white checkered floors were shined enough to see themselves in. Marble columns held the building up on the foundation and the walls and countertops were trimmed in gold. They stepped onto the elevator and Lance pushed the button for the twenty-eighth floor.

Cali wondered out loud, "Lance, what is up on the twenty-eighth floor?"

He smiled at her impatience, "Just a little more and you will see." He began kissing her lightly along her collarbone to distract her as much as possible but it wasn't working. Cali couldn't hide her anxious energy and was beyond bewildered. He kissed her once more, this time on the lips; "Shut your eyes."

Questioning everything, "Shut my eyes? Why? Lance just where are we going?"

He was hardly holding in his laughter as he thought he should record this moment; "Dear, please just shut your eyes. Trust me, okay?"

Taking a deep breath, she did; he took her by the hands and all the while reminding her to keep her eyes shut. When they got to the door he stated proudly, "Okay, now open them!"

As her eyes adjusted to her surroundings she saw her name on the door; a gold plate, Dr. Cali Evans; Private Psychologist.

Lance held her from behind, "You can see by the last name on the door I would have done this for you even if we hadn't gotten married."

It still hadn't fully dawned on her yet; she asked, "This is my office?"

He reached underneath the mat and discovered the keys the realtor left for them and gave them to her. She stood there holding her keys to her heart with tears flowing freely, "When did you do this? How did you do this?" She opened the door and fell back in Lance's arms; hugging him with all of her might. Her office was decorated with all of her favorite colors; a beautiful peach colored couch in leather made the centerpiece of the waiting room along with leather multicolored pillows in ivory, mauve, and brown with drapes to match. Cali opened the drapes; the view of downtown took her breath away; it was what she'd always imagined. She had windows surrounding the entire office; natural light flowing from different angles.

Cali hugged her husband again, so emotional from this surprise, she couldn't stop crying. "I know I'm truly loved. God loves me to send me a friend, a lover, a billionaire and he's handsome. If this is the kind of love I can expect being married to you then I'm goanna need some weights to keep me from floating away." She closed her eyes with a smile as bright as the sun. "Lance, you are truly amazing."

Lance loved doing for others; giving without expecting anything in return, a trait he'd picked up from his mother and grandmother as a child. He simply leaned against the wall and watched her continue touring her new office. Cali walked around touching everything as if she was in dream. Everything was made especially with her in mind, no more little cubby hole in the basement with broken drawers and no filing cabinets or storage space shared with three other people. Rushing back towards the front she called out, "Wow, just wow, now I have an actual sitting area; my own office that I can close the door to and a kitchen where I can even cook if I feel like it." She gasped as she ran her hand over the countertops, "Some people would kill for this kitchen." She continued to familiarize herself, noticing there were three bathrooms and a second office; with its own bathroom.

Cali ran excitedly into his arms and kissed him lovingly. He reciprocated with a fierceness of his own; passion building as fast as it had started. They caught themselves before going too far. Cali mused, "I can't believe there was so much thought into buying this place, all the way down to decorating it. I know you weren't here because you were with me but somehow you were still able to oversee everything. You captured all of me. How was it meant for one person to be so lucky?"

Lance intertwined his fingers with hers; "You mean two lucky people. Let's go home so we can finish what you started." He grabbed for her hand to lead the way. As they were leaving Cali paused one last time, smiled into the reality of her new office; her mind already thinking ahead of what she had to get done from hiring her small staff to building her client list. She wiped another tear before she turned out the lights and locked the door behind them.

Chapter 20

They arrived outside of Lance's condo; Cali couldn't wait to get unpacked and settled so she could call Meghan and let her know she was back. She also needed to find out if there was anything else to be done for her wedding. Having been away from her best friend for a week, he was sure she was anxious to call her and tell every single thing that's happened; so he busied himself in the kitchen as she put away some clothes and dialed Meghan's phone number. She found herself willing her to answer the phone as she listened to it ring on the other line.

"Hello." Meghan answered sleepily.

"Wake up chick! I'm back!" Cali spoke excitedly into the phone.

"This can't be my girl calling me!" She exclaimed coming fully awake. She pushed herself up off of the pillows her honey propped up behind her before going to the gym.

Cali exhaled heavily into the phone, not sure where to begin. "Yes, Meg; it's me! We just made it home not long ago but I couldn't wait to call you. I'm calling to see if there's anything else we need to do before your big day."

Meghan thought for a moment, "Everything is done. The only thing I need is for you to try on your gown to see if we need any last minute alterations because you may have eaten like a pig on your vacation." They laughed together at her joke; Cali still glanced at herself in the mirror to see. Meghan continued, "Oh my god Cali it's felt like you've been gone for a month."

Cali chuckled, "Yeah I know. It's only been a week, but it did feel longer; so much has happened."

Meghan heard something different in her voice; "Oh really now? So, tell me; how was your trip? And you better not leave anything out missy."

Cali took a seat on the side of the bed. "Meghan, all I can say is I came back because of my best friend's wedding."

Meghan hollered and rubbed her belly, "Girl, get out!! You had such a good time you almost didn't come back?" a pregnant pause danced across the sound waves before she continued. "Well, did you?" Cali was puzzled. "Did I what?"

Meghan yelled, "YOU KNOW WHAT I MEAN. DON'T PLAY DUMB WITH ME."

Cali's stomach cramped, she laughed so hard and said in a whisper, "Yes, girl; over and over again." they both screamed like two high school girls. Lance heard Cali's laughs all the way in the kitchen and could only imagine just how much information she'd divulged to her friend; he didn't mind though. Hearing her laughter caused him to chuckle as he placed the chicken into the oven to broil.

Meghan calmed down enough to finally speak again. "I can't wait to see you. I've missed you my friend."

"I've missed you too." Cali stressed. "I will be down town tomorrow at the licensing bureau trying to get my license switched over to private practice. Let's get together for lunch.

"That's right; you did mention you were going into private practice, are you ready?" Meghan asked.

Cali stuck out her chest, "Meg, I can only take it one step at a time and I will have more control over the type of clients I see, not like at the hospital."

Meghan asked, "Have you heard from Jena's mother or anything about her case?"

Cali answered thoughtfully, "No, not yet, but before we left on our trip I heard she got a lawyer. I know I'll hear something soon."

Meghan wanted to know more; "Does Lance know you're going into private practice?"

"Oh yes, he knows."

"Wait a minute." Meghan paused. "Why did you say it like that?"

Cali promised, "I'll tell you all about it when I see you for lunch."

"Wait." Meghan said, "You just can't leave me hanging like that." She whined.

"I'm going to get some sleep. I haven't slept since we got in. Love you Meg; I'll talk to you tomorrow." She yawned loudly.

As she moved to press the end button on the phone, Cali laughed as Meghan yelled, "Boooo you suck!"

* * * * *

Later that night, Cali and Lance were deep into a love making induced sleep when Cali suddenly sat up in bed shaking so; it woke Lance too. Worried, he asked, "What's wrong? Did you have a bad dream?"

Her chest heaved in and out; it took her a moment to respond. "Yes." She sat up. The gown she has on felt cool and sticky against her clammy skin; she was soaking wet. Lance went to the bathroom to get her a towel to dry off. He kneeled before her and helped her wipe herself. Cali stopped and looked him in the face. "Lance, I don't what anything to happen to you."

Lance moved to sit next to her on the bed. "Why do you think something will happen to me?" He held her face; leaned in touch her forehead with his own; "Cali, baby talk to me; what did you dream?"

She opened up, "I had this same dream the night before Jena died."

Lance asked, "Jena, your patient, right?"

She nodded, "Yes. The night before she died I had this very same dream about a boy who was yelling for help."

"Where was he when he was yelling?" Lance wanted to know.

Cali added. "It was on one of the floors of the hospital. It was weird because it sounded like a little boy and then the voice kept getting older like a young adult. So I went into the room where I heard the yelling and it was a young guy in his hospital gown, covered in blood. When I went to ask him could I help him and what was his name; he answered Cali."

Lance sat back in confusion. "What?"

Continuing with the telling of her disturbing dream; she stated again, "He said his name was Cali, the same as mine. I just ran out of the room to go for help and I ran into Dr. P, the doctor that did the surgery on Jena's baby." Her head hung low, her voice just above a hoarse whisper. "Lance I never told you, but he was the doctor that delivered me and he was in the dream; I asked him to come back to the room where I had seen this kid. He went back to the room with me but no one was there. The alarm woke me up. By the time I'd made it to work Jena had killed herself." Her shoulders felt like concrete had suddenly weighed them down. "Lance, I have never dreamed anything like that before. I don't want anything to happen to you or Meghan. I feel like something is going to happen."

Lance had never seen Cali this emotional about anything. He tried to reassure her, "Nothing is going to happen to me. Don't worry okay?" He made her get up from the bed and took her to the shower. He gently instructed. "Come on, get in."

"I still have my gown on." She fussed.

He said, "So, that's fine." and stepped in the shower with his pajamas on. He pulled Cali in with him and as he always did he helped her get through this stressful situation. She couldn't help but laugh as warm water streamed. "You are just completely crazy, but that's why I love you."

Lance hugged her, "Cali you are my wife and I won't let any happen to you. I love you too."

They tossed wet clothes and they hit the shower floor. They made urgent love in the shower; one thing that could calm them both down. Cali towel dried her hair and waited for Lance to make them some chamomile tea. She felt relaxed enough to go back to sleep.

The next morning as Lance got dressed for work he asked, "Will you be fine? I can have someone else cover my rounds for another day if you want me to stay home with you."

Waving him away, she said, "Oh honey, yes I'll be fine. I have so much to do myself; like go file for my private practice license and stopping by my apartment to get some things. And then meet up with Meghan for lunch to touch base about her wedding."

He watched her as she answered, "Okay, but if there is anything too heavy you want to get out of the apartment just leave it and I'll get it for you later." He kissed her goodbye and went about his day.

*****

Cali's mail box was full to the max from being gone; but she got the letter she was expecting; it was a letter from Jena's mother's lawyer asking that he talk with her concerning her death. She opened up her curtains and windows to air out her place. Checking her phone, she noticed she had seventeen messages on her answering machine and they were all from her mother telling her she needed to talk with her. Cali sat down on the couch for a moment; looking at the phone trying to decide whether or not to call her mother. She didn't want to engage in any kind of conversation that usually ended up nowhere, but she didn't want something to be wrong; she still decided to hold off on returning her call. Cali muttered to herself, "I swear if mother talks about Dr. P I'm going to tell her what I think of her and Dr. P."

Against her very will and with much regret Cali couldn't resist, she dialed her mother's phone number. Cali tried her best to muster up some jovialness, "Hi mom, I saw you called. I just got back into town from the Bahamas. What's the matter?"

Cali's mother seemed nervous to speak with her. She'd never heard her mother sound so out of it before. Something in the pit of her stomach gave her a foreboding feeling she couldn't explain. "Mom, what's wrong? You sound strange. Is dad okay?"

Her mother replied, "Oh no, honey, he's okay." She swallowed hard.

Cali pressed. "Then what did you want to talk with me about for you to call seventeen times? It must be pretty important."

Cali's mother continued to dance around the subject of why she wanted Cali to call. Trying to change the subject, she asked, "How was your trip? I hear the Bahamas is beautiful."

"Nice." Cali answered and her eyes widened in shock that her mother asked her something about her for a change. "Yes mom, the trip was very nice. So nice in fact, I didn't want to come home."

Her mother hoped talking about the trip would make her forget about her messages she'd left. "Did you go with your man friend?"

Cali silently huffed. "Mom, his name is Lance. And yes, I went with him."

Her mother asked her, "Um, Cali, I need to talk with you about something very important. Can you come over?"

Cali was losing patience, "Mom, is this in reference to Dr. P again?"

"Yes but," she stammered and before she could further explain why it was concerning Dr. P Cali exploded, she said, "Mom, I just knew we couldn't have a conversation without bringing up Dr. P. What is it you have to tell me, huh? Is that why dad left? Were you having an affair with him? Am I his child?" She fired each question at her mother, not giving her a chance to answer. On a roll, she went on venting. "Well, let me tell you about your Dr. P. By the way, his name is Dr. Peter Martin. He is the blame for my patient jumping out of the window."

Cali's mother had heard about a young lady committing suicide, but she had no idea how close to home this was. "What? " Oh my God."

"Yes, your precious Dr. P changed the sex of my patient's baby. She didn't want him to nor did she give her consent and she killed herself. So do you think I want to talk any more about Dr. P?"

Cali's mother answered in a very low defeated voice, "I guess not." She thought to herself of how after years of being afraid to tell Cali the truth, this latest news has made it impossible to tell her. All she could think to say was, "I'm sorry about your patient Cali. I'm truly sorry."

Cali immediately felt sad for talking to her mom the way she had. She'd never talked to her so disrespectfully but thought she should know what he'd done.

Her mother broke the silence that had suddenly engulfed them. "Well, I'll talk with you another time Cali."

Cali still didn't have her answer, "Mom, before you go I still want to know; did you have a relationship with Dr. Martin?"

She answered with so much conviction, her mother's voice made her jump in surprise. "No! I have never cheated on your father!" Cali felt somewhat relieved to know that her mother did not have an affair; most importantly he was not her father. Cali asked pleadingly, "Mom, please never badger me about seeing Dr. P again."

Her mother answered as if all of the wind had been knocked from her lungs, "Okay, I will never bring his name up to you again."

Before hanging up Cali decided to tell her mother the most important news of the moment in her life, another surprising blow, "Mom, I got married while I was in the Bahamas." She smiled as she thought of Lance.

Her mother, stunned, "You did what?"

Cali repeated, "Yep, you heard right; I got married. And when you're ready I want you to meet him. He's a doctor and a truly wonderful man, mom."

Cali's mother sat stock still in shock, married; Cali was married. Her words reverberated in her mind like church bells. She found her voice and croaked, "I'll tell your father and congratulations, I hope you will be happy."

That was not what Cali expected to hear from her mother. She wanted to hear her say something like, "I'm so happy for you my daughter; bring our new son-in-law over so we could meet him" but Cali knew her whole life was full of disappointments so why should this be any different. The phone call ended with both upset and in tears. Cali sat and cried; a pain renewed from her youth, feeling even a marriage could not pull her family together and her mother's tears of guilt; missing the one chance to tell her daughter about her past was lost. She felt she would not have the courage to ever bring it up again especially not with the way Cali felt about Dr. P.

Chapter 21

Cali's mother regained her composure and called her husband. She told him she needed to talk to him and it was very important he come to the house as soon as he could. Mr. Evans knew it had to be important; he'd never heard his wife sound so distraught. He told her he would be right there. He threw his shirt on haphazardly and grabbed the keys to the car in one move. The drive home was difficult. It seemed the longer it took the more nervous he became. He prayed nothing was wrong with Cali.

Finally, he'd turned onto the street and spotted their driveway. Memories of how he wished it had been flooded his thoughts; he fought back emotions as he killed the engine and moved to go inside. He found his wife sitting in the living room in complete darkness. He called out to her timidly; she answered, "I'm over here."

"Why are you in the dark? He asked with growing concern as he stumbled around trying to find where the lamps were to turn them on. The only light glimmered softly from the kitchen and only reached so far into the living room. When he finally clicked on a lamp and saw his wife he could tell she had been crying and she looked as though she had been wearing her night gown all day.

Mr. Evans stood next to the sofa; "What is wrong?" He longed to reach out and hold her, but it had been so long, he was sure any form of intimacy would be turned away.

She mumbled, "I tried to tell her but it was too late."

He said, "You tried to tell who what?"

Mrs. Evans stared at her husband, her voice flat. "I tried to tell Cali the truth about who she was but it was too late."

Mr. Evans said nervously as he slowly sat next to her on the couch, "Why now after all of these years that you want to tell her?"

All of the pent up emotions she's felt since doing what they'd done came up and out; Mrs. Evans yelled at her husband for the first time since they were married and said, "Mike did you ever see how unhappy our child was! I guess not because you were so busy making sure you weren't here. You didn't hear Cali cry at night, but I did! I didn't want to tell her until she was grown, but I see even now was the wrong time; she should have known a very long time ago! I was her mother and even though she didn't talk to me I could see she never felt uncomfortable with who she was. I let her go on thinking she was doing something wrong when she wanted to wear boy clothes, but Mike no matter what the doctor did to change her physically, she was a boy and she had the right to wear them. Can't you see? We distorted almost everything about what she was born to be and when she didn't act the way we wanted her to act we made her feel like something was wrong with her, but it was really something wrong with us! We separated as a family and left her to believe she was the cause of it and when she started to act like a women I couldn't even be happy for her then and now she's gotten married!" She stopped short on purpose to give her next statement greater affect; "To a man!"

Mr. Evans covered his face with his hands in disbelief and stood up. "She got married? When and to who? Does he know who she is?"

Mrs. Evans answered as best she could. "I don't think so. Not yet anyways, but when he does find out, how is Cali going to feel? And how is he going to feel knowing he married a man? At least if Cali knew she could have entered into a relationship with someone accepting her for who she really was and if we had told her sooner about our reason for changing her maybe she would be more forgiving, but at this point I don't think we can tell her now."

Unshed tears found their way down the face of a soldier. His own father had told him it was unmanly to cry, but that day he cried for their son. He fell to his knees and asked his wife to forgive him for everything.   "Honey, I need you to understand, I didn't leave you because I didn't love you. I've never loved a woman more than you, but I changed our baby. You depended on me to make the right decision and I made it out of pride."

Mrs. Evans cried with her husband. "We did it together. Don't blame this all on yourself. I had my hand in this too."

Mr. Evans was determined to shoulder all of the guilt, shaking his head adamantly. "No, I am the blame. When Cali was just starting to walk, I saw my son; I saw the boy in her and when she would come to me wearing those dresses I couldn't see picking up my son with a dress on and I was too ashamed to come to you and say we may have a problem, but instead I left you to deal with all of this and until this day I have not held my child or let her know just how much I love her. He laid his head in his wife's lap and sobbed; still begging for her to forgive him.

She caressed his head with a blank stare. "I have always forgiven you Mike I just hope one day our child will forgive us."

*****

Cali, tired from wallowing in her own grief, got up to go to the bathroom. She washed her face and thought back over the conversation she'd just had; even though she was sad, her conversation with her mother did not bother her as much as it used to. As she washed the tears from her face she saw a new life with love and made up her mind once and for all there would be no more tears because she had someone she could talk to and who cared about what she thought or felt did matter. Her phone rang and it was Meghan calling about their lunch meeting. Cali told her she was just leaving her apartment. Meghan told her to go ahead and just meet her at the bridal shop for her final fitting so any last minute alterations could be made. Cali quickly gathered the things she'd come to get and took one last look around her apartment. She'd miss her little quaint place; she knew she would never live there again.

Cali walked towards the entrance of the bridal shop and watched Meghan waddle her way in her direction. Funny the difference a week made; Cali thought upon seeing her best friend, she should be the one getting refitted. Hugging and kissing as if they hadn't see each other in a year; Cali teased, "You sure I'm the one who needs to be refitted? Gees' woman! This wasn't here before I left."

Meghan laughed along with her; glowing from her pregnancy and her pending nuptials. "Yeah, I know right? And don't worry I've already taken care of that. With the way she made my dress I'll have room."

Cali was glowing for an entirely different reason; she couldn't wait to see the look on her friend's face when she told her the news. Meghan suggested, "Hey, let's grab lunch so we can catch up after this dress fitting is taken care of. I want all of the details of your trip and don't hold anything back. You cheated me yesterday, but today you spill it all."

Cali knew she'd held out big time and crossed her heart as she laughed; she had more to tell her than she could even imagine. Cali's maid of honor dress was even prettier than she remembered and she thanked God she hadn't gained any weight; the dress still fit perfect. Cali ran her hands down the sides of the dress while admiring herself through the three sided mirror. Meghan couldn't help but notice a sparkling light coming from Cali's finger. She slowly snuck up on Cali like a cougar on his prey, then suddenly grabbed her hand and yelled; "Ooh MYY GODD!! CALI YOU DIDN'T!"

Cali smirked as she shook her head and said, "Girl, yes I did!" Happy screams were heard throughout the bridal shop. Cali had not planned to let Meghan see the ring but had forgotten to take it off before she left the house; the secret was out now.

Meghan rushed her, "Hurry up and take that dress off. We need to talk now." They walked down to their favorite spot, Ruby's Bar and Grill. Meghan requested to sit in the area where they served the drinks because she knew most people, when they drank they normally didn't pay attention to other people's conversations. They couldn't sit down fast enough before Meghan grabbed Cali's hand again; this time to really inspect the ring. She marveled, "Aww, Cali this is so beautiful! Did you pick this out yourself?"

Cali shook her head, "No Lance had this before we left for the Bahamas. He told me he'd already planned to ask me to marry him. Besides you know me; I would have never picked out something this big."

Meghan agreed, "And big girl it is. Now that I have caught my breath and I'm somewhat over the shock, tell me how did everything happen?"

Cali settled into her seat and went on to tell her about their trip, "Let me tell you; as we drove up this country road there was this beautiful house sitting off in the distance near the beach. I told Lance how much I liked it. It was then he surprised me, he told me that it was where we were going. Meghan he actually owned the house, had maids, and ground keepers that keep the place up when he's not there. I got the chance to meet the nanny that raised him. She was so sweet and made me feel so at home. But wait a minute, whoa, let me back up to the very, very beginning; he gave me a choice of three places to take a trip to begin with; he has properties in all three places. He treated me like a queen and I could not hold back on him any longer. When we made love we both could not stop our chemistry; it's so unbelievable it's almost scary. He asked me to marry him on the island all out of the blue. I wanted you to be there so bad, but I knew you would be happy for me either way. I didn't want to tell you about my marriage until you had yours though, but you, deputy dog who notices everything; I had no choice."

Meghan smiled broadly, "Cali I am so happy you finally found someone to love and trust and he's pretty handsome too."

After they wiped their tears away Cali admitted, "But Meghan, we have one slight problem though."

Meghan sat forward, "What is that?"

"Lance is a billionaire." Cali stated quietly.

Meghan looked as though she was about to choke, she grabbed her glass of water and took a swallow. Cali patted her on the back, "Meghan, are you alright?"

Finishing her swallow, she spoke into Cali's face, "Did you say billionaire; the one with the "B?"

Cali nodded, "Yep, the one with the "B"."

"Wow. Did he make you sign a prenuptial agreement?"

Cali answered, "No, he said that everything he has is mine."

Meghan still couldn't believe it. "Oh My goodness Cali; so what are you going to do? I don't see him being a billionaire being a problem at all if you ask me."

Cali agreed, "I plan to live like I have been living. I asked him how come he never had a body guard. He said he's a doctor first and he can't take a body guard in his patient's room and I agree with that. He says if you don't draw attention to yourself you can live a normal life like anyone else. Even though he said if I want something I can buy it, but you know that's not me. I told him I am in no way giving up Burger King or MacDonald's just because I'm married to a man with money now. "Megan said "Oh hell yeah, Burger King and McDonalds stays. They then burst into laughter know how silly they sound and drawing a few looks from nearby tables.

After they finished lunch Cali told Meghan she had some place to take her. The entire ride there she kept asking, "Where are you taking me?" Cali just drove on in silence with a mysterious smile on her face.

The doorman recognized Cali and welcomed her back as he opened the door for them to enter the high rise building. Meghan begged, "Cali these are offices. Come on; spill it, where are we going?"

Cali laughed as she recalled how she carried on with Lance just the day before; "Gosh, Meg, I've never seen you so impatient." They stepped into the elevator, arms linked jovially and Cali pushed the button for the twenty-eighth floor.

On the ride up Meghan joked, "And they have music in here too. I guess they don't want you to know that you're going as far as heaven."

Cali laughed, "You are so crazy. Hang tight, we're almost there." The elevator doors opened and they began the walk down the hallway towards her door. Cali pointed to the door and announced, "We're here."

Meghan stepped closer and read aloud, "Dr. Cali Evans, Ph.D. Psychology." Turning to Cali, she said, "Don't tell me this is your office! When did you do all of this?"

Cali pulled out her keys to unlock the door, "I didn't; Lance had his realtor find this while we were in the Bahamas. I didn't see it until we came home; he surprised me." When Cali opened the door Meghan's eyes bulged out like child brought to a candy factory. Cali began to get emotional all over again herself.

She managed through her own tears, "Cali this is the most amazing thing I have ever seen and what make it so spectacular is that someone thought enough of you to do this for you." She beamed at her friend as she made her way through touring the space. "Now you have your own office and look he even paid attention to you and knew your favorite colors. I thought I was the only one that knew them."

Cali hugged Meghan, "Now, do you see why I love him so?"

Meghan took a seat, "Honey, he had me at the trip to the Bahamas, but Cali your ring, this office, and he turned out to be a billionaire with no prenuptial agreement. Cali this is a man I can say truly loves. You will always have his heart."

Cali hugged Meghan again, crying, "I know."

Meghan sat back and arched her brow, "Now aren't you glad we went to The Topple that night? Boy, wait until I tell Doug."

"Meg, can you please leave out the fact that he's a billionaire? That part still has me a little nervous for him. No one here knows that about him."

Meghan promised, "I won't tell him about that; it'll be our secret."

Holding onto her hand, she gave a grateful nod, "Thank you Meghan."

*****

When Cali made it back home Lance was already cooking dinner. Cali came in all smiles, "Hi honey, you're home early and something smells good."

Lance replied, "I just put on some steaks and I picked up a bottle of wine. How was your day? Did you get your license changed over?"

"Yes, it was fairly easy. I thought I would be there all day but I was in and out. I went by the apartment to get a few things."

Lance interjected, "Is there anything I need to get?"

Kicking off her shoes and burrowing her toes into the thick Berber carpet, she offered, "I boxed up what I wanted. We can go by later this week and pick them up. I figured I'll just donate the furniture; I'll call Goodwill so they can send someone to pick them up." Taking a moment to pour a glass of wine for each of them, she continued. "I also got a letter from the attorney for Jena."

Lance cut his eyes at Cali with a raised brow. "Well, you did sort of expect that."

"Yes." She muttered as she taken her glass of wine and walked back into the living room to settle into the sofa. She spoke quietly. "I talked to my mother today."

Lance yelled from the kitchen; "What did you say honey?"

Taking another swallow, she spoke up. "I talked to my mother today."

Lance came out the kitchen wiping his hands on the dish towel looking a little worried because he knew every time Cali talked with her mother there was drama. He sat down next to her, "Well, what happened?"

She took a deep breath and another swallow of wine before answering. "When I checked my messages I saw she'd left like seventeen messages while we were gone and she had even called Meghan looking for me. So . . . I called her to make sure she was okay and to find out why she'd called so many times. She said she had something to tell me. When I asked her was it concerning Dr. Martin she said yes. Lance I couldn't help it; I lost it. I asked her did she have an affair with him and if that was the reason my father left and of course she denied it and asked me how I could even think that. I told her the only thing she's ever talked about to me was that damn man so what was I supposed to think.

Lance had never heard Cali curse. He knew she was getting really upset; he began rubbing her back as he spoke gently, "Calm down."

Cali nodded, "You're right." She took another deep breath. "Well I told her all about her precious Dr. Martin and what he'd done to Jena's baby. She was surprised and I asked her to never bring that man's name up to me again." She told me, she would never bring his name up again. Cutting her eyes at Lance she continued. "I also told her I was married."

Lance sat up straight, curious to hear her mother's response. Cali took too long to answer. "Sooo, what did she say?"

She stared pitifully ahead with tears making treks in her foundation. "Congratulations." She shook her head and snorted in disgust; guzzling the half glass of wine. "All she said was congratulations."

Cali looked like life had dropped out of her. Lance wrapped his arms around her shoulders. "Don't be sad honey. She's never met me and I know if she did she would love me." He put his hands under her chin and made her look at him. "What's not to love about this face?"

She couldn't help but smile. "I am sure it's not you. This has been going on long before I ever met you I just wish I knew what "this" exactly was."

Lance stood and pulled her to her feet. He gently kissed her. "Come on, let's have dinner."

Cali followed him into the kitchen, "Honey, I'm so sorry. You did all of this and I'm not that hungry. Meghan and I grabbed a bite after stopping by the boutique for last minute alterations to my gown."

Smiling as she remembered her friends reaction, her mood did a three sixty. "And baby, let me tell you; I forgot to take off my ring. She noticed it with her nosy self and flipped." She ended laughing.

"Was she upset?" Lance asked concern.

Cali answered with zeal. "Meghan was very surprised, but very happy for me. I also took her by my new office; she was as shocked as I was and told her that's why I love you because you truly love and care about me."

Lance glanced lovingly at her as he fixed himself a plate of food. "I will always take care of you and I will be there for you when you need me." He grabbed the bottle of wine and said, "Let's sit in living room since you're not hungry." Cali grabbed her half full glass and a television table for Lance. He made himself comfortable, spread a napkin over his thigh, said a silent prayer of thanks, and watched Cali get comfortable in between sips of wine. "Well, my dear, you're not the only one who had an exciting day."

Cali looked surprised; Lance never complained or talked about anything unless it concerned her. Cali was happy he had something he wanted to talk about that concerned him for a change; then guilt pricked the bubble of happiness as she realized she'd never really asked him about his days or his feelings. As she prepared to listen to whatever he had to say she made a promise to herself to stop being so self-absorbed and caught up in her own issues.

He revealed to her he was offered the position of Director of Medicine at Langley Hospital. Shrugging his shoulders in between bites, he went on to explain; "I decided to finally except the position because they've been trying to get me there for a while but it wasn't until after the incident with you that I said yes. I want to work at a place where my wife can come see me and not have to rehash all of the things that went on and besides it hasn't been the same since you left."

She was feeling warm and fuzzy from her glasses of wine which made her all the more emotional; she looked over at him with a hand to her chest; "You did that for me?"

Pausing to think and take another drink of wine; "Well, yes." He smiled as Cali sat down her drink, moved his dinner tray to the side, and got on her knees in front of him start to un-belt his pants. This sudden move had Lance momentarily stupefied; this wasn't something she was used to doing other than when they were in bed. Cali undressed Lance and showed him just how happy he made her over and over again.

Chapter 22

The next morning Cali had an appointment to see Jena's attorney to give her statement. She walked into his office with faux wood paneling and a dented receptionist's desk. The coffee pot percolated like an old truck motor in the corner. She tried to make herself comfortable on the plaid sofa and thumbed through an old magazine. Returning his call after her trip was not a problem for her; she wanted to help bring justice for Jena any way she could. The door to the office she assumed was his; was closed. She was beginning to get anxious; ready to get this meeting over with. Suddenly, the door swung open and a mousy young woman with dull brown hair shuffled toward the couch with papers falling to her feet as she sat down. Nervously, she nodded hello towards Cali and adjusted her glasses with a nerdy push up on her nose. The attorney hired by Jena's mother appeared in the doorway hooking his thumbs around his suspenders; rocking back on his heels he took a moment to appraise Cali before calling her into his office. He apologized for her wait and didn't waste any more time with getting into his questions. Just by her statement he knew her testimony would be a key piece to his case. He told her as she prepared to leave that she would be subpoenaed.

Glad to have that part of her day taken care of Cali called Meghan to see how she was feeling and to find out if they had picked out the cake; with her wedding coming up the following Saturday Cali didn't want her to have to worry about needing anything at the last minute. Meghan assured her everything had been ordered. Feeling satisfied Cali she bid her dear friend so long and thought to surprise Lance so she could see his new office. When she got there a very pretty lady greeted her from the receptionist desk. She slung her head of shiny red hair over her shoulders as she reapplied her MAC lip gloss. To Cali, she should've been walking someone's catwalk; her antennas went up instantly.

Cali asked in a syrupy voice, "May I see Dr. Roberts please?"

The lady looked at her with a little carouse and protected look before answering. "Who shall I say you are?"

A new emotion began to rise in Cali's chest; jealousy. She'd never had to face a woman who may be interested in Lance; she was going to have fun with her. She replied with a bit of haughtiness. "I'm his wife. MRS. Roberts."

The lady looked as if she'd spilled grape juice on herself and her face reddened, easily showing her embarrassment. She quickly said, "Oh I'm sorry Mrs. Roberts! I didn't know the doctor was married."

Cali smiled at her with squinted eyes as if to say, "I see all through you", but instead she said, "How could you have known; he just started today."

The receptionist muttered, "Yes, you're right. I'll let the Doctor know you're here."

"Thank you so much." Cali answered as she took a seat in the waiting area.

Lance came out instantly to meet his wife. He excitedly hugged her and led her back to his office. He had not finished setting his office up, but he did have their wedding picture in the Bahamas on his desk. Cali picked it up and stared at the picture still trying to accept that she was indeed married. He asked did she want anything juice or water to drink? She shook her head no; explaining she'd just stopped by to see his office and where it was located. Closing the space between them she wrapped her arms around his neck as they shared a kiss filled with so much passion; Lance had force himself to remember he was at work. He pulled away and she told him she wasn't staying long because she was going shopping to get some things for her own office. He walked her to the elevator and kissed her again. "Be safe. I'll see you at home."

On his way back to his office the receptionist said to him very flirtatious way, "I didn't know you were married."

Lance stopped short and asked, "What is your name again?"

Not sure where his line of questioning was going she said, "Patty Phillips."

Continuing, he probed, "Is it Miss or Mrs.?"

"It's Miss." She replied regretting she ever attempted to flirt with him.

Lance explained to her with a stern voice. "Ms. Phillips, to answer your question; yes I am married and when my wife comes in she is to be referred to as Dr. Roberts as well."

Patty knew she could not play those games with Lance as she had done the previous director. She quickly answered, "Yes sir Dr. Roberts."

"Thank you." Was all he'd said as he turned on his heel and made his way back to his office. He did not want to appear to be a bad guy but this kind of behavior was not going to be tolerated so he felt compelled to nip her forwardness in the bud. She had no idea she was dealing with a pro at those games after dealing with countless nurses and women doctors. He was fully content he'd found someone who wanted him for him and not because he was a doctor. Just looking at the pattern, she was flirty with him and had not known whether he was married or if he had a steady girlfriend; the only thing they knew was he was a doctor and that would give them instant status from being with him. Lance was not going to allow these types of goings on to be a part of his work space nor would he allow his wife come in a guessing game atmosphere where she would even think is he sleeping with his receptionist or anyone else for that matter. Lance shut the door to his private office as he shook his head and smiled. He was confident he'd put an ending to what would have been a very unhealthy office atmosphere.

He settled in to his seat to review the Simon case file and called Patty to bring them in to him. She brought the files in swiftly and asked him if anything else was needed. He smiled and answered no. To himself he said, "That's the professionalism I want to see." As she closed the door behind her he rubbed his hands together and opened the file to view his first case.

*****

Cali found herself enjoying her shopping excursion. She'd purchased everything she needed for her office; only thing was missing was a television. Even though she didn't like being extravagant she had a very beautiful, but quite large office and would need a nice sized television to take up some space; a little television just wouldn't do, so she took the dive and made a big purchase. She began browsing all the while thinking of just where she would have a fifty inch installed on the wall in the waiting area. It felt good to know she'd be making the purchase it with her own money. Even though she had access to Lance's bank account and all his credit cards she did not want to spend his money; besides he had already gotten the office for her and paid to have it decorated; she figured she could at least buy some things for herself. Before she had access to Lance's money she felt she was well off any way because she had all ways saved and invested; one thing she and Meghan did so they would have money after they finished college.

As Cali looked around for a television there were lots of programs on just to display the quality of the picture but one in particular caught her eye. It was a program on about people who felt they were in the wrong body. As Cali listened to it, old insecurities crept up and wrapped its arms around her shoulders like an old friend. She heard testimony after testimony of people not knowing who they were and then finding out they were changed when they were babies and their parents didn't tell them; some of them were married and their spouses found out and left them and some of them were even badly beaten by their spouses. Watching made her start to feel sick to her stomach. One of the store associates noticed Cali watching the program and made a very negative comment about the people on the show and what he would have done if someone he'd married was not who they said they were.

She pushed past him to run to the bathroom to empty her stomach. She stared at herself in the mirror; it seemed that years of programming herself to who she was were gone. She washed her face and started to leave the store when the store associate asked her was she ready to purchase a television. She answered quickly, "I'll be back another day."

The store associate was puzzled because he knew that was a for sure sale. He stared curiously at her wondering what could've happened before answering, "Okay, but when you come back here's my card; just ask for Alex."

Cali took his card and didn't even look at it; she just looked dazed and said numbly, "Okay Alex."

When Cali got home she jumped into the shower and stayed for what felt like hours. She toweled off and climbed slowly onto the bed. She tried to understand why her thoughts were so screwed up. She had everything going for her and now she was back with her childhood problems and what was worse now she didn't have Meghan to talk to, or so she thought. She didn't want to bother her with issues they both thought were dead and gone. She was getting married Saturday so she resolved she'd have to pull it together for her.

Cali noticed she had a voice mail from Lance reminding her of how much he loved her and that he would be a little late and if she wanted him to bring something special home. She smiled at the sound of his voice telling her to give him a call. Her chest swelled with love as well especially when she heard him say, "Oh heck, just call me for the hell of it. I love you. Talk to you later." That message sent Cali balling; she thought of how it would feel to lose him, but more importantly how would he look at her if he ever found out about how just how much she'd dealt with growing up; feelings of being a boy trapped in a girls body.

Later that evening when Lance came home he knew Cali was there because her purse was in the chair but all the lights were out. He thought that was strange. He yelled for her then he finally went into the bedroom. She was in the bed curled up beneath the covers. He sat on the side of the bed with her, with worry in his voice he wanted to know, "Babe, are you alright?"

Cali answered somberly, "Yes, I'm alright."

Rubbing her back he pushed forward, "Did you get my message?"

"Yes, I got it." She apologized. "I'm sorry I didn't call you back. I needed to lie down a bit."

She was starting to scare him a bit and he was a man who didn't scare easily. "Um, why are you in the dark?"

"I'm resting my eyes."

The energy between was limp; He wanted the fire and passion back. "Well, I want to see your beautiful eyes."

She didn't want him to see she had been crying and told him, "No." She said while grabbing his hand as he tried to turn on the bedside lamp. "Just get in bed with me please and hold me."

He thought that was strange. He knew the way she was acting, something was definitely wrong. He took off his clothes and climbed into bed with her. Something in Cali wanted to prove she was all-woman by making love to him. She climbed on top of him and took control. Lance absolutely loved Cali's sex, but she just kept going and going; he couldn't keep up with her. Out of breath he managed, "Baby let me catch my breath a moment."

She climbed off of him and laid with her back to him in a fetal position. He kissed her back, making himself comfortable next to her. "I know something is bothering you, but I will give you time to talk to me. When you're ready just know you can talk to me about anything and Cali I mean anything. You are my wife. Now, you are my life."

As Lance held her the tears flowed from her eyes.

*****

The next morning Lance didn't want to leave Cali's side, but she told him she would be fine. He didn't need to be taking off from his new job so soon. She didn't want him to miss any days.

He lovingly reminded her, "Have you forgotten; I don't have to work when it comes to you? I will give up everything."

She held her husband's face, "I know you will, but you are a doctor. Now go to work. I promise I'll be fine."

He begrudgingly replied, "I'll call you later to check up on you and if you need me for anything just call me and I'll come right home."

Cali still in her bath robe dragged herself into the kitchen to make some coffee and reassured him, "I'll be fine honey, I promise."

Cali could no longer play these guessing games. She needed to know if she was a man or a woman, but she wanted to be seen by a doctor in another city. She thought of the doctor who'd helped those people on that television program and she Google the show to find his name. It took her a few moments of staring at the phone number before working up the courage to finally call. Her intentions were to just ask some questions before she made any kind of appointment. When she called she was expecting to talk to a receptionist, but a man answered instead. A little startled, she asked, "Is this Dr. Owens' office?"

The man on the other end of the phone replied, "Yes this is Dr. Owen."

Cali froze. She didn't know what to say next.

Dr. Owens used to people's apprehension from first callers searching for help probed, "How may I help you?"

Cali shook herself from her stupor; "I'm sorry I was surprised you were answering your own calls."

She could feel him smile warmly through the phone. "Yes I feel it works better for my client's privacy."

Cali yelped, "Yes, that's great!"

Dr. Owens patiently asked, "How did you find out about me?"

She took a quick breath, "I saw your program yesterday. Can you briefly tell me exactly what it is you can do for your patients?"

Dr. Owens stated matter-of-factly, "I will try to sum it up for you. I work to help people who are having problems identifying their sexuality. What kind of problems are you experiencing?"

For the first time ever she spoke openly with her answer, "Just what you mentioned. I have had these feelings since I was a child and I thought I'd gotten over them, but looking at your program brought those feelings back with a vengeance. And now I feel worse than ever because I just got married and I have never discussed this with my husband. I can no longer ignore these feelings. I have to know what I am."

Dr. Owens spoke up, "May I ask you what sex are you living physically as right now?"

Cali answered, "As a woman"

"Why did you choose a woman?"

Cali answered in a slightly raised tone of voice, "Because I have a vagina."

Dr. Owens said apologetically, "I didn't mean to upset you. It's just I have some clients who have a penis but feel like females."

Cali shook her head as if he was there in the room with her, "No, I'm the one who's sorry. I am just nervous and very sensitive about this; I just want it to go away."

"Well you sound like a good candidate. When can you come in for a consultation?"

Cali found the courage to take the step she said she wanted to take. "Dr. Owens I don't have time to sit on your couch to have my head picked, I need some actual physical proof of what I am."

Dr. Owens explained, "My program has three phases. The first phase is your consultation. The second is an actual physical. The third phase is the results and an outcome planning."

Anxious, she asked, "Can we just skip to phase two? I feel like I have just been through phase one."

"I understand the urgency you may be facing, but this is how this program is set up. What I could do to speed things up is to schedule your consultation and physical on the same day."

She physically sighed with relief and took a cleansing breath; "That would be perfect."

She made an appointment for Tuesday the twenty- second well after Meghan's wedding. After Cali hung up from talking to Dr. Owens; the phone rang and it was Meghan. She was so happy to hear from her; she knew if she had no one else in the world she could talk to and who would understand without judgment; it was Meghan. Cali told her that she needed to talk to her and asked if she could come over. Meghan answered, "Sure! You know you're always welcome!" "I'll be there in an hour." Cali hung up with mixed feelings but the depression that had suddenly set upon her the day before was slowly shifting towards definite peace.

Chapter 23

When Cali arrived at Meghan's she was sitting out by the pool; even though she was pregnant, she still looked good. Meghan immediately noticed Cali was worried about something. She asked, "Do you want something to drink?"

"Sure do. A glass of wine will definitely do."

She fixed Cali a glass of wine and poured herself a glass of milk; her latest craving.

She sensed her friend was in serious need of a hug. "Cali, what's wrong? And don't tell me it's nothing. I know you remember."

Cali finished off her glass before agreeing with her, "Meg, yes I remember, but do you remember those nights I used to cry to you and tell you I didn't feel like a girl but more of a boy?"

"Yes." She said as she recalled the sad young girl she helped pull out of her insecure shell.

Cali continued, "Well those feelings are coming back again."

Megan asked, "Why? You have been doing so well? You have an adorable husband that loves you. And you're getting ready to open your very own practice!"

Staring off into the horizon, a bird flew across the sky and sparkled in the sunshine. "I know, but I saw this program on television the other day and it had these people talking about how they felt and they got answers."

Megan sat forward with interest. "Okay, I'm with you so far."

Cali stated, "It is this doctor that does a little counseling with you and then he helps you get a physical to find out your sex. And he also helps you get through the result process."

"Cali, I don't understand. Let me get this straight; so he gives you a physical. Don't you have a vagina? Why would someone have to test you?"

Cali went on with her explanation. "Do you remember Jena's son being turned into a girl? Well, what if no one tells him he was born a boy and he ends up feeling like I do? How would he ever know?"

Megan reasoned, "But your mom."

Cali cut her off, "Yeah, that's right; my mom. Look how she and my dad act toward me and I know there is something they are not telling me about my past and I'm also sure this had something to do with my parents separating. Meghan no one will be happier than me to find out that this isn't true. And maybe this is the real reason I have not had a period and not some bullshit about I was so athletic. Meghan I haven't been an athlete in nine years, so now what's the excuse? Meg I need to know, this marriage is new and I don't want to wait until Lance is asking for children and we find out that I'm really a man."

She tried her best to think positive, "Cali don't talk like that. Of course you're a woman. I've seen you naked; we have the same looking lady parts."

Cali mused, "I know but that is the worst it can get; I have set up an appointment after your wedding to go get checked out."

Meghan reached for her hand, "Do you want me to go with you?"

"No, girl, you'll be on your honey moon."

Meghan said, "I'll postpone it. Doug will understand."

Cali was adamant, "Not this time sis, I have to do this myself. And to be honest I'm ready to find out."

All kinds of questions worked through Meghan's brain but the main one found its way out into the open; "Aren't you worried about Lance and how he'll react?"

The heaviness returned to her chest. "More than you could ever know. He is such a wonderful guy. I would do anything not to hurt him; my only regret would be I didn't try to find this out sooner." Cali began to choke from the emotion and said, "I'm sorry to lay this on you right before your wedding but I knew afterward you'd be on your honey moon and I would not be able to tell you. Plus I really needed to get this off of my chest."

Cali and Meghan held each other and Megan always finding the humor in everything said to Cali, "I don't care if you find out that you're triggers lost uncle on his father side you'll still belong to me."

Cali laughed as she thought, "Only Meghan."

Meghan laughed along with her at her own silly joke. She looked at Cali seriously, "Did you hear what I said?"

Cali stopped laughing and looked back at Meghan, "Yeah, Meg I heard you."

Meghan said in a teary voice, "Remember Cali, no matter what happens we're family."

Cali felt a little better, "I know that things will be alright. God sent you into my life and then he sent Lance. Why should God stop now?" Standing up to leave, Cali said, "Now, let's put these tears away and get ready for this wedding."

*****

She went home and fixed Lance the most scrumptious spaghetti dinner he ever tasted; at least that's what she was hoping. She'd picked up some garlic rolls and red wine on the way home. When she got home, a gentlemen was about to leave a note on the door. Cali asked, "Can I help you?"

He turned around to greet her, "I'm looking for Dr. Cali Evans."

Cali answered, "I'm Dr. Evans; how may I help you?"

He pulled out a subpoena, "Sorry ma'am, you're being subpoenaed to court for the case of Jena Shepard vs. West Wood Hospital."

"Thank you." She called out to his retreating back. Cali took the letter and opened it, she was shocked to read the court date would be so soon; the next Friday on the twenty-fifth; looks like she would have one busy week after the wedding. Cali went inside the apartment and started fixing dinner for her husband; she did not want him to come home to another gloomy day. After she finished cooking she took a shower and but on a sexy blue lounge dress. Cali heard Lance coming in. She hid behind the door and jumped out, "Boo!"

Lance laughed heartily; she'd really scared him. He thought he was going to find her still in her bathrobe looking and feeling bad. He presented her with some flowers and a diamond bracelet. When she opened the box up she said, "Lance, what is this?"

He said, "If this didn't make you smile then I know what ever was bothering you is pretty serious."

"No lance I don't want you buying me expensive gifts like this when I'm not feeling well. Flowers would do just fine honey. But this is a beautiful bracelet."

Lance loved how she was so different from other women he'd met, "I can take it back if you don't want it." He chuckled while watching her.

She had already started putting the bracelet on her wrist. The five carat diamonds didn't need sunshine to gleam and shine; they shined on their own. She relented, "No; no that's okay this time but remember next time flowers will do." They laughed together, touching foreheads; she gave him a big kiss. "Thank you, honey."

Lance shrugged it off as if no big deal, "You're welcome baby! What smells so good?"

Cali replied coyly, "We're going Italian tonight."

"Whatever it is it sure smells good." I'm going to get cleaned up so we can eat he threw a towel over his shoulder as he walked towards to bedroom to get in the shower.

Cali set the table and lit some candle lights to create a nice ambiance. When Lance got out of the shower he noticed the letter on the dresser and called out to Cali, "Hey baby, is this the subpoena for Jena?"

Cali came into the room, "Yes it is; this guy was leaving it today when I came home."

He inquired, "So when is the court date?"

"It's next Friday, the twenty-fifth."

As he dried his hair he looked at her leaning against the dresser; "Are you nervous?"

Cali crossed her arms over her chest, "No, I will just tell the truth."

Lance smiled proudly, "That's all you can do; tell the truth. And one more day is Meghan's wedding."

Cali pushed herself from the dresser and sat down on the bed, "Yes, I know right? Now I am nervous for that."

He wondered aloud, "Why?"

"Because I know she will be nervous which will make me nervous."

Lance said, "Well, you didn't look so nervous when we got married." He pulled her back to her feet into an embrace.

Cali swooned in his arms, "Lance, we were on an island with strangers; I didn't have to walk down the aisle and hope I don't trip then. Come on let's go and eat."

At the table, Lance said, "Well babe, see how much agony I save you?"

Cali threw a piece of lettuce at him and said, "Sit and eat you mad man." As they ate and laughed Cali thought for a split second of what she would do if she had to tell Lance she was a man. Not only Lance; but how would she feel herself knowing she had women body parts.

Lance watched Cali wandering mentally from their conversation; he waved his fork in front of her face, "Are you with me?"

Cali smiled, "Yes, I was just thinking about the court date."

Lance looked over to her and said, "Don't worry about that; you're with me now."

He helped load the dishwasher and used that time to also load her with compliments; telling her how the dinner was unbelievable and she looked beautiful in her blue lounge dress. Cali turned to him, "Take me to bed."

Lance kissed her on the neck, "You don't have to ask me twice."

She stepped into the bedroom and allowed her dress fall to the floor; she had nothing on as he laid her onto the bed. Cali turned herself onto her stomach suggesting to Lance the way she wanted him to make love to her. She remembered the only time they made love this way was when they first got together. As Lance penetrated her from behind she released an oozing sound pleading with him to go deeper. He wanted make sure he was not hurting her, but from her body movement he could see she was enjoying every inch of him. Granting her wish he pushed deeper. They moaned together in sheer ecstasy; Lance ran his tongue along the center of her back and rubbed her breasts; he could never see himself without his Cali.

Cali felt Lance thrusting passionately in and out of her. Her climatic scream paired with the declaration of her love drove him over the edge. She panted over and over again, "Lance! I love you! Lance! I love you!"

He climaxed with her amid his own screaming, "Ohhh Cali, I love you too!" Their bodies still sensitive to touch made them tingle well into thirty minutes afterwards; they didn't want to remove themselves from each other, holding on to every nuance of their lovemaking. When they did pull apart, they lay in each other's arms and slept.

The next morning Lance didn't want to leave but Cali, as usual, reminded him of his duties so begrudgingly, Lance went off to work. Cali pushed herself up to get moving herself to get some last minute things for Meghan's wedding and to pick up Lance's suit. Cali kept thinking about her mother and feeling guilty about their last conversation. So much so, she decided to pay her a surprise visit.

She knocked on the door and waited patiently for her mother to appear. She was astonished to see her father answer. She looked at him with a strange expression; totally thrown off of why he was even there. She asked blandly without saying hello or bothering to ask him how was he doing. "Where is mom?"

His heart dropped a bit, he said, "She's in the kitchen." He realized Cali was still looking at him strangely, as if to ask him, "What are you doing here?"   But her mother came out of the kitchen looking happy and relieved to see her.

He'd stepped back for Cali to enter as she went to her with concern, "Mom, are you okay?"

Nodding fervently, her mother replied, "Yes, yes; I'm glad you came by. Did you bring your husband with you? We'd love to meet him."

Cali couldn't get over how happy her parents seemed; this was something she definitely wasn't used to and even asking to meet Lance, she answered, "No, he's at work." She was leery and continued looking at her mother like, "Okay, when is the drama going to start?" But she didn't say anything, just smiled back at Cali as she made her way into the house. Then Cali thought maybe it will be dad with the drama, but he didn't say anything either. Cali was starting to feel like she was dreaming and she would eventually wake up; she was definitely in a twilight zone.

Cali said, "Well mom I just dropped by to see how you were doing." She turned to head right back out; this was too weird, seeing her mother and father; together. As if they were the normal kind of family.

Her mother spoke hurriedly reaching for her, "You're leaving? Can you stay? You just got here."

Cali thinking of any excuse to leave spoke shakily, "Meghan's bachelorette party is tonight, I have to make sure everything is ready for that and I have a few other errands to run. We're all excited her big day is finally here tomorrow."

Her mother remembered, "That's right it is tomorrow. Please tell her congratulations again for us."

Cali tried hard not to flinch when she heard "us". "I will." She started on her way back to the car again. Her father called out, someone had to take the first step toward some semblance of a relationship he figured; "Your mother told me you got married, I hope he's good to you."

Those words sounded like a stranger was speaking to her; she couldn't remember her father saying more than five words to her. He walked over to her and hugged her, saying, "Cali, I love you, I've always loved you. Please find it in your heart to forgive me." He backed away with his head bowed.

Cali was so thrown off with everything happening she started bolting for the door as if to say, "Who are these people?" She yelled over her shoulder to them; "I'll call you."

As she drove away deeply disturbed and unsure of how to process this latest encounter; she thought of the years she wanted to hear her father say those very words; of how much he loved her and how much she longed for him to hold her in his arms. Although it took a long time for him to tell her he loved her she still believed in her heart he meant it. Cali felt a sense of closure had just then taken place and made up in her mind she would no longer worry about why he left. She had gotten the real answer she had been seeking anyway; and that was knowing if he loved her. Cali knew she could not expect a person to tell you everything no matter how close you were to them. This made her mind wander to Lance, she knew she was withholding information from him, but she loved him with all her heart. And even though her mother didn't announce it out loud, she knew her father was home again and her mother would not be alone. She felt the difference in the atmosphere as soon as he opened the door; he was there to stay. She was glad to see the smile on her mother's face and know they had each other again. But . . . that foreboding feeling still lingered; mixed with her happiness as she tried to toss it out of the window of her worries.

Chapter 24

Later that night was Megan's bachelorette party and Doug's bachelor party. Cali called Lance as she laying out her outfit to remind him of Doug's party.

Lance was preparing to finish up his early day as he answered her, "Yea, Doug had already called me."

Staring at herself in the mirror she contemplated trying something different with her hair and make-up, "and to have a good time."

Lance laughed while telling her, "I will and you too but don't do anything I wouldn't do."

Cali cackled and spoke to him in a very coy tone, "But my dear Lance you do everything."

Lance arched an eye and felt his nature rise but calmed himself down; they'd have enough time for that after the parties, but he remembered hearing stories of what all went on in those bachelorette parties and it made him a little jealous to even think of another man touching her. He got up from his desk and began pacing back and forth as he continued their conversation, "Well, let me change that then. Don't do anything unless I'm doing it to you."

Cali smirked and said, "Visa versa Mr. Roberts, see you when I get home. I'm packing my things to get dressed at Meghan's house."

Lance smiled into the phone, "Don't get home too late you need your beauty sleep."

Cali replied, "Yes dear."

She thought it was cute how Lance sounded a little jealous. She grabbed her bag and keys to head out as she recalled Meghan said she had a surprise for all the girls in her wedding party. Everyone met at

Meghan's house where she had a limo waiting. They made a toast with champagne and snacked on light hors d'oeuvres as the traveled to their destination. Meghan wanted everyone to feel their best for the wedding and the food was very good but healthy; nothing fattening.

They were taken to a spa that was like no other spa they'd been to. After a detoxifying shower they were given pedicures and facials. All of the women were enjoying the pampering session; so much so some even said it felt better than sex. Cali and Meghan said unison, "I don't know what kind of sex you're getting!" Laughing and high fiving each other as the other ladies joined in the laughter.

They thought they were being taken to a room for their nails to dry; it was a beautiful room with palm trees in every corner and a mural on the wall of a tropical island with enough massage tables for all of them. They were asked to lie down and make themselves comfortable on the table of choice. When they thought things couldn't get better; from a hidden doorway, an all-male masseuse team came in to give massages. It was the best massage any of them ever experienced. The evening ended with class and a group of slightly drunk women.

When Cali made it home Lance was still wide awake. He had not been apart from Cali since they were married. Cali was feeling rejuvenated and wasn't ready to go to bed yet even though it was pretty late. She had a busy day ahead and a lot to think about. Lance came out of the bedroom to see if she'd had a good time.

Cali gave him a quick rundown, "Yes I enjoyed myself. It was very nice. We went to a spa."

Lance looked a little happier, "Oh that does sound nice. I guess Meghan didn't feel the need to have raunchy strippers and all; she did her thing with class. I like that."

Cali was careful not to include there were male masseuse. She didn't want to take that happy look off of his face. She tilted her head with a little curve of a smile, "Well?"

He stared innocently, "Well what?" He knew what she wanted to know.

She wanted to know how rowdy they'd gotten and wondered if he'd tell her. "How was your party?"

He shrugged and sat down on the sofa, "Eh, the usual, dancers; food; and drinks."

Cali chuckled at how boring he tried to make it sound. "I thought men got tired of that kind of thing."

Lance propped his bare feet on the coffee table, "Men never get tired of that."

Cali cut her eyes at him, "So, were you excited?"

Lance admitted unashamedly, "Yep, I sure was." He loved watching her try to control her reaction to his answer. "I was excited about getting home to you."

Cali leaned over and kissed him lightly on the lips, "Good answer baby."

He beckoned her with a wave of his hand to come to him; he pulled her down onto the couch and made love to her. Watching the strippers jiggle and shake at Doug's party had him more than ready.

*****

The next morning, the big day Meghan and Doug had been waiting for; with the wedding set for two o'clock that afternoon Cali didn't want to eat, but she still wanted to cook breakfast for Lance. He turned down a hot home cooked meal, opting for something light himself; he told her he'd just make himself some cereal.

Cali laid her gown out and Lance's suit and went to run the tub for a nice little bubble bath. When she stepped into the steaming water and placed warm cloth over her eyes for a moment before finally laying her head back. They had a tub big enough for two people, which is why she didn't feel him when he slid in to join her.

Lance was there for about fifteen minutes and he took this time to watch Cali's face make all kinds of expressions. He interrupted her meditation touching her feet. She jumped up, "Oh my god Lance you scared me."

He said, "I have been in here with you for about fifteen minutes and you didn't even move. You smiled for a while and then you looked to be sad." Finally working up his nerve to ask; "Where do you go when you're not with me?"

Cali sat up and splashed a bit of water his way, "What do you mean? I don't go anywhere."

He said, "No, I'm talking about mentally. Where do you go? Where ever it is, I feel left out of your life. I feel like there is something you're not telling me." Sitting up himself he reached for her hands underneath the water, "Cali, I know we rushed into this marriage, but I thought we felt the same about each other. Is that what it is? Are you having second thoughts about marrying me?"

Cali leaned forward, "Oh, no Lance. We do feel the same way about each other and you should know that I would not let anyone rush me or push me into anything I didn't want to do. I do have something on my mind. But I can't talk about it right now. After next week I promise I will tell you either way good or bad."

He relented, "Okay, I'm not going to pressure you. I'm going to trust you on this, but the end of next week Cali I want to know you're my wife; wholly."

Cali tried to lighten the mood by pinky swearing, "Yes, I promise."

They finished bathing and out of the tub and dry off. She sat at the dresser to make herself up; she'd decided to go a little heavier on the eyeliner and mascara for a more dramatic look but light on her blush and lipstick. The affect was breath taking; this was the prettiest Lance had ever seen her. She glanced back in the mirror to look at him when she got dressed; she looked more like the bride to him, giving Lance a glimpse of a moment he took from her; a woman's wedding day. Lance paused while putting on his cuff links to ask her, "When everything is over; the wedding, Jena's trial, and your issue you're going to tell me about next week, can we have a formal wedding with all the trimmings? Looking at you so beautiful in that gown made me realize you missed out on a dream wedding; a woman's dream wedding."

Cali's heart warmed with a deepening love for her husband and his desire to keep her happy, "Lance, I agree, yes that is a woman's dream, but if you think about it, I had a dream wedding too. I had a beach side wedding with the mother earth as my canvas with the sands beneath my feet, tropical music, the most handsome man I have ever seen, and a diamond ring that would make even Elizabeth Taylor jealous. And to top it all off, you go all out to give me anything I want; what more can a girl ask for? Lance, baby, my friends don't know it, but I am officially a queen. Even Meghan knows I have hit the jack pot with you. I overheard her telling Doug he needed to take notes from you." She laughed softly before continuing.

"I'm sorry you're feeling that you've done something to make me feel this way , but please believe the only thing I can tell you is I wish that I had straightened something out before we got married. But we're going to be okay."   She walked over to him and kissed him gently, careful not to smudge her make-up. They stood together admiring each other in the mirror, looking like a couple out of a magazine. As always, they complemented each other. She turned to him; they looked into each other's eyes and kissed again. Realizing it was time to head out, she grabbed her clutch purse and they left for Meghan's wedding.

When they got there, Cali left Lance to help Meghan finish getting dressed. She was a beautiful bride; belly and all. Her auburn hair set off her cream colored gown. The gowns lace top fell off of her shoulders and the corset looking waist line made her look very slimming, even in her second trimester of pregnancy. She was illuminating; the bridal party agreed Doug would be thrown when he sees his bride. Cali looked at her friend and thought back to when she first met her and knew that her life would not have been as fulfilling if she hadn't come into her life. She had so much to thank her friend for. Cali and Meghan looked at each other, each feeling nostalgic and both agreed no crying until after she gets married; no one wanted to mess up their make-up.

As everyone got in place, the organist started playing the wedding march for them to make their grand entrance down the aisle. All Cali could think about was how Meghan's marriage was beginning and how hers could possibly be coming to an end. She didn't want to feel so negative, but she'd rather prepared for the worst and wait to rejoice if she ended up getting the best. She turned at that moment to look at her husband; he whispered, "I love you."

She whispered, "I love you too."

Just as Meghan came down the aisle, Doug burst into tears from her beauty. As she got closer to the podium tears streamed from underneath her veil as well, her initial promise now a memory at seeing his reaction to her. It touched her all the way to her soul. Once they'd exchanged vows and pronounced man and wife; Meghan grinned broadly, she was officially Mrs. Meghan Silverman."

The reception was as classy an affair as her bachelorette shower had been; Cali reached for Lance's hand to dance with him. They danced non-stop and had a good time. Meghan and Doug were about to leave for their honeymoon but hated leaving the party; she gathered all of the single ladies to catch the bouquet and Doug gathered all of the single men to catch Meghan's garter. He gained a lot of cat calls when he lifted her dress and pulled it down her leg with just his teeth. Meghan fanned herself like some southern belle while her eyes spoke volumes to him of what they'd be getting into as soon as reached their destination.

Before they could leave, Meghan took Cali into a private room to talk with her for a few minutes. She told her, "Now, don't say a word. Even though I'll be on my honeymoon I'm still going to be checking with you about your results." Cali moved to interrupt her. "Nope, I don't want to hear it. Just know I love you sis."

The stress of her pending appointment finally broke Cali down; she cried because her friend would not be there to go through this with her and the fact she didn't want Lance to know; feeling this is something he just would not understand. Meghan shook her gently by the shoulders, "Be strong! Even though you love someone, you still have to be true to yourself first." Cali dabbed at her tears and reapplied her lipstick so Lance wouldn't see she'd been crying and start worrying about her again.

*****

Cali enjoyed the rest of her weekend with her husband; they went to the movies, opera, and dancing. Cali simply wanted to spend all of her free time with Lance. They even met for lunch that Monday. That heavy foreboding feeling made her feel like everything they were doing was for the last time.

Tuesday arrived, but only Cali knew how important this day was. She had to go see Dr. Owens; it was a two hour drive and her appointment was set for eight thirty that morning. She left Lance sleeping, but wrote him a note that she had an appointment and had to be there early; writing she would be back before lunch. "At least that much is the truth." She thought as she kissed him on the forehead and left.

When Cali walked through Dr. Owens office doors he was a little taken back because sometimes he could tell whether someone was a man right away, but he couldn't with Cali. He had her answer the rest of his questionnaire. And then he sent her down the hall for her physical. Cali would finally find out the truth. They took blood samples and performed a rectal and a vaginal examination. Cali thought if this didn't tell her then she was going to be a woman without any more questions.

She went back to Dr. Owens office and he explained the results would be ready in two to three days and he would call her upon receiving them. Cali and Dr. Owens shook hands and Cali headed back to the city in a daze. As Cali drove back to the city she knew in her heart what the results were. She had even thought about riding off the bridge so she wouldn't have to hear them or hurt her precious Lance. What kept her going was the yearning to hold on to the good life while it lasted because she was definitely facing an uncertain future. She powered her cell phone back on the closer she got to the city limits and noticed Lance had called her several times. She called him back to let him know she was home.

He chided, "Babe, you had me worried. You'd left while I was a sleep."

She said, "Honey, I left you a note, didn't you get it?"

He replied, "I still wished you would have waked me up."

She wanted to reach through the phone and smooth his brow she pictured all wrinkled with worry for her, "Lance you were sleeping so well. I didn't want to disturb your rest."

Lance became curious about her sudden disappearance; "The place you went today, did it have anything to do with why you have been so sad and worried?"

Cali answered, "Yes."

Lance took a deep breath, "So Friday, you're going to tell me what you been keeping from me."

Cali confirmed by saying, "I made you a promise and I don't break my promises."

Signing some paperwork, he asked one last question, "Will you be home when I get there?"

She told him while kicking off her shoes to get comfortable, "Yes, I sure will. I'll see you when you get home."

There was a moment of silence before Lance finally said, "Cali, I love you."

"I love you too." Cali pressed the end button and tried to shake some happiness back into her bones.

Lance walked through the door being greeted with his slippers and robe. She'd even prepared his bath water just the way he liked it; and frankly he knew he could use it a nice soak after the day he'd had, the busiest since being on his new job. She kissed him and took off his jacket then his tie. Lance had already unbuttoned his shirt as he walked to the bedroom. Cali could see Lance was still a bit upset and that made her nervous, in all the time they've known each other, he'd never been upset with her. But then again, she hadn't given him anything to be upset about. She tried to sound nonchalant, "Lance are you upset with me?"

He turned to face her while getting undressed, "I have to be honest with my feelings; yes because I have to wait until Friday to find out what's going on with you. Do you know how that makes me feel Cali; do you really have any idea how I feel?" Lance walked into the bathroom and settled down in the bath tub. He laid his head back to rest his self and to calm down; he knew that he had never been this angry with her before. He just laid there hoping the hot bath would relieve the tension he felt.

Cali sat in the living room thinking of ways she could tell Lance the truth, but technically she didn't know the truth. It wasn't something like honey I've over drawn our account or I had an affair. All of these sounded better than honey I think I'm a man. It was no way she could bring herself to tell him and risk their marriage without being absolutely sure. She stood up suddenly, got her purse and left. She could not sit in there knowing she was making him feel so bad when all he ever did was try to make her happy. Lance heard the front door open and close. He hurriedly got out of the tub; slipping and almost twisting his ankle; he grabbed his robe and yelled out for Cali. Silence answered back. She was gone. He ran to the door to see if she was perhaps just standing outside but she wasn't there either.

Lance sat on the bed with his hands covering his face. He didn't know where to begin to look for Cali. Meghan was on her honeymoon; so he couldn't call her to see if she was there with her; he felt helpless. He thought maybe she'd gone back to her place but immediately remembered she couldn't go back to her old apartment because she had already given notice to vacate. Where ever she'd gone off to she had no plans on staying out all night because she knew that even though Lance was upset with her, he would still worry.

In her car, she rode in silence with the windows down. The night air was as soothing as a lullaby. She ended up going to her office and started putting away some of the things she'd purchased. She cleaned the entire office to keep from thinking about Lance and her test results. She was glad the place was dusty; this made her have to really focus on getting it clean. When she was almost finished cleaning she heard a knock on the door and it startled her; she couldn't think of who would be knocking on her office door this time of the evening. She wasn't even open for business yet.

She stood at the door and asked, "Who is it?"

She heard Lance's voice. "It's me Cali. Open the door please."

Cali opened the door up looking as dusty as the office she'd just cleaned. Lance walked up to and hugged her. "Cali I am so sorry I made you feel you had to leave home."

Clearly tired and worn out from worrying about her test, worrying about Lance and having to go court for Jena, she felt she was coming apart at the seams. "I couldn't bear the thought of you being mad at me. You have always been there for me and for you to be that upset I knew I had taken your patience with me to another level. Lance when I met you I had never dated because there were things about me that has haunted me since I was a kid. I couldn't talk to anyone but Meghan, but as a kid I needed professional help. I had no one to help me get it. I know I've told you about my relationship with my parents. I didn't get around to telling you that my father told me just the other day that he loved me. Do you believe that out of twenty-six years this is the first time he'd said he love me?

Lance interjected, "I understand but I keep telling you, now you have me. Honey I love you."

Cali held her palm up, "Lance, let me finish. I have to get this out before I lose my nerve. I had no support to help me deal with these feelings I had no one but Meghan. We were kids trying to deal with a grown up problem. That's why I chose to study psychology; I wanted to self-diagnose and self-medicate. Then, I met you and things started to change. I felt good about myself. You were handsome, nice, and patient with me. I fell in love with you and when you asked me to marry you I thought I would be nuts to let someone like you get away."

Lance couldn't stop himself from asking her, "What happened?"

She continued, "It was the day I went shopping for my office supplies. I went in the store to buy a television and a program was on with people that were suffering from the same thing I've been going through and for some reason my old haunting feelings resurfaced again. There was this doctor that had help these people come to terms with these feelings and then go back and face the family. That's where I went today. I had to go see him. I wish that I knew about this type of program sooner but I know I won't be a complete wife to you until this is over.

Lance was still confused with what "it" was that had her going to see the doctor, but asked thoughtfully, "It will be over by Friday?"

Cali nodded affirmatively, "Yes, I will get the answer by Friday."

Lance shook, "It's sad that a problem you suffered with almost all of your life would have only taken a couple of days to solve." He stood up and reached for her. "Cali, come on home and get cleaned up. I will wait for your answer honey with no pressure. You will never have to leave our home again."

When Cali had left the house she hadn't worn a jacket and the night air was a little cool. Lance noticed her shiver and took off his jacket and put it across her shoulders. Making it back home she headed straight for the shower to wash off the dust and all of the misery of the day. That's how she always tried to wash away her sadness is with a shower and somehow she did feel better. While she was in the shower

Lance made her a cup of tea and a sandwich. He brought the sandwich and tea to her in bed. He told her he had to go out for a minute and would be back.

She looked up at him and whined, "But Lance it's late out."

He kissed her on the forehead, "Honey, I'll be right back; in less than an hour." He left quickly before she could try to convince him not to go. He went to his office and gathered some files he knew he needed to look at that following morning. He grabbed another set of files to keep him busy at home for a few days. He knew one thing for sure; he was not going to leave Cali's side until this thing with her was over. He left his secretary a phone number where he could be reached. He was glad he had taken this position because it allowed him to work from home. He decided it was a perfect time to begin using this particular perk. Cali was asleep by the time he made it back; he knew the chamomile tea would put her to sleep. He took off his clothes and climbed in bed with her. He held her as if he thought she would run away.

Lance woke up early that next morning; he wanted to study his file before Cali woke up. She got up to go to the bathroom and noticed Lance was not in the bed. She panicked thinking he hadn't come home all night. She walked through the living room looking frantic. She noticed the light on in his office. Knocking on the door, she felt her heart begin to slow its pace. She opened the door and saw him sitting at his desk. "Were you in here all night?"

He kept typing and still spoke without losing his train of thought; "No, when I got home you were sleep. I got in bed with you but that tea had you really sleep. I just woke up about an hour ago so I could go over these files."

Cali took a seat in the chair and crossed her legs, "Lance you're going to be tired by the time you get to work."

He stopped typing and smiled over at her, "I'm going to work from home for a couple of days."

"Awe, honey, you don't have to be here with me."

He waved her words away, "But I want to be here with you. And I want you with me so it was easier for me to bring my work home than have you to sit in my office, don't you think?"

As he went back to typing on his computer she asked, "Can you do that?"

He stopped again and looked at her and laughed, "Yes, I could have always worked from home and now I need to do this and besides even if I couldn't; nothing would stop me from being here with you. Do you think I could have gone to work and concentrated on my job, not knowing what's going on with you?"

Her head cocked to the side; "I'm not a baby."

He continued his work, "No you're not; but you're my baby."

She came over to him and kissed him. He was so tempted to pull her robe open but he needed to finish a report first. She offered, "Well, least I could do is fix you some breakfast."

"What would you like?" He then requested, "Just coffee, eggs and toast."

Cali didn't want to admit it but she was actually glad he was home and she was glad that he was really getting some work done. She realized his discipline was phenomenal; he only came out of his office to refill his coffee or to go to the bathroom. As lunch time rolled around, he took an extended break to eat with Cali. After a two hour lunch he told her he would be finishing in a couple more hours. For the next few days that was their schedule, Lance remained by Cali's side.

Chapter 25

The next morning Cali was to report to court. She made sure she was looking professional. After she finished styling her hair, she noticed Lance getting ready too. "Are you going to court with me?"

Lance answered, "Of course, did you think I would leave you today of all days?"

Cali remembered this was also the day she would find out about her results. It was an eerie feeling to know these results may change her life. Then Cali thought, "Hmm, what if I don't take the call? I don't have to. Lance and I can continue living our lives together. As a matter of fact, I am going to call the doctor and tell him I don't care what the results are I want him to destroy them. I don't want to lose my husband." Cali was about to call and tell the doctor to just forget about it.

Lance's voice pierced her thoughts and intentions, "Come on Cali. You know you can't be late."

Cali then planned to call him when she got to the courthouse thinking she'd have a couple of minutes but ironically it started on time. She felt very aggravated she didn't get a chance to call the doctor. She resolved internally, "When he calls I'll tell him I don't care and hang up. That's all." That whole morning felt gloomy; Lance could feel it too. He mentioned he felt like he was going to a funeral and it wasn't because they were both wearing dark suits. Cali was dragging even more, she knew by the time they made it home she would hear the results of her test. But she didn't care; she was not going to end her marriage.

They held hands and found a seat; Cali saw the doctor's sitting at the table with their lawyers. She really didn't care if she never saw any of them again, especially Dr. Martin. When the Doctor's noticed Cali they all turned around and looked at her as if seeing a ghost; turning back into a huddle around the table they started whispering."

Cali waved and smiled at Jena's mother; they were not allowed to actually talk to each other for now. Cali did briefly speak with the lawyer as to what to expect and when she would be giving her statement. Cali and Lance sat in the back next to the door because they wanted to get out of there as soon as she was done doing what she had to do.

When everyone was settled in the court room; the bailiff called out in a deep clear voice, "Everything to order." The judge entered; his black robe billowing about his feet made him seem as if he was floating. The hospital went on the stand first with their big time attorney's trying to jump all over the legal system but Cali prayed to God they would not prevail. Dr. Martin took the stand claiming there was no record of Jena saying she did not want her baby's gender changed. He also claimed he thought the baby was abandoned by the adopted parents giving the baby back to the state. And how they called the state and gained permission to operate on the baby. His lawyer said he had no further questions for Dr. Martin. It was time for Jena's lawyer to ask Dr. Martin his questions. "What happened to the baby's genitals that you had to order this kind of surgery?"

Dr. Martin was speaking as if he was purposely trying to muffle his words so the jury couldn't understand him. But the lawyer made him repeat himself. Dr. Martin answered, "The baby's penis was burned during a circumcision."

The lawyer then asked Dr. Martin, "Are you sure you weren't trying to cover it up the fact you burned this baby's penis knowing you may have to pay compensation to the mother?"

The hospital's lawyer called objection to his line of questioning. The lawyer changed his line of questioning but made them wish they hadn't objected. He asked Dr. Martin, "How many surgeries have you order like this?"

He bragged and stated proudly, "Maybe about a hundred."

Cali could not believe that many children were changed and that's not to say about other doctors who were probably doing the same thing. The lawyer said incredulously, "Dr. Martin, do you mean that many children you have burned their penises?"

Dr. Martin looked shocked upon realizing what he'd just implied with his answer. His lawyer attempted to object again. Jena's lawyer shook his head sadly and said he had no further questions for Dr. Martin. He then called Jena's roommate to the stand. He asked her to tell what she knew.

She explained how she had just been admitted to the hospital that Friday. Jena had had her baby before she did. That Saturday Jena was arguing with that doctor and she pointed to Dr. Martin. They're lawyer sounding like some type of trained parakeet yelled objection again but the judge allowed her to finish answering the lawyer's questions. She said she heard Jena telling him not to change her baby and the doctor said he was going to call the state people. She was so upset after he left. She tried to call Ms. Cali that night. After she left a message we walked down to the nursery to see our babies. My baby was there but Jena's wasn't; she kept knocking on the window asking for her baby and they told her to see the doctor in the morning. One nurse was kind of rude, she told her the nursery was closed and pulled the curtain closed. The next morning Jena kept trying to reach the doctor but he never came to see her then she heard one of the nurses say they changed her baby. Jena started screaming and crying. The nurses came into the room and tried to calm her down. Nothing worked. They even told her she was going to break her stitches. She screamed she didn't care and then they gave her something in a needle. When she woke up she just kept mumbling about how he was her child; her responsibility; and how they had no right. I was upset too. I just want to go to sleep and get me and my baby out of there the next morning which was that Monday. The nurse came and woke me up asking if I'd seen Jena and I said no. I went turned over to try to go back to sleep and that's when the nurse noticed the window was open and the curtain blowing. She ran over to it and looked out of the window and she started screaming. That's when I knew Jena was dead. Rehashing the entire experience brought forward emotions she thought she'd moved beyond. She started crying, as well as few of the women jurors.

Dr. Martin dropped his head. The next witness called was Jena's mother. Her lawyer asked her nicely, "How are you feeling?"

Months of grief made her shoulders sag as she spoke. "I keep thinking Jena's going to walk through the door. Sometimes I have to remind myself she's gone."

He asked her to tell them if the baby was doing fine. She could barely speak. She just flagged her hands and said, "Sir that baby has a vagina but he looks like a big strong boy, it's just not right. That boy is not a girl!" She was inconsolable and had to be escorted from the stand. Cali got teary-eyed as well as some of the other people there listening. After Jena's mother's statement the lawyer told Cali he may not need her statement. She was glad but then surprised to hear the doctors lawyer call her to take the stand. Cali and Jena's lawyer both wondered what they could possibly want with her. He had to know she could only hurt their case.

When Cali took the stand they began asking her did she speak with Jena about her baby. Cali said, "Of course we talked about her baby."

He asked, "Did you encourage her not to change her baby's gender?"

Cali sat as straight as a board, "No that was her choice as I noted in her file."

He then asked her, "What did you ask the nurse?"

Cali slightly cleared her throat, "When Jena told me about them wanting to change her baby I had never heard of such a thing. I thought maybe she did get the doctor's intention right so I went to ask her nurse so I could fully arm her with the facts. By the time I came back to her room she was telling me she didn't want her baby changed she wanted him as God made him and she wanted to keep him; she no longer wanted to give him up for a adoption."

"Dr. Evans."

Cali corrected him with pride, "The name is Dr. Roberts now."

"Oh my apologies, Dr. Roberts; you didn't like these baby changes; isn't that the reason you encouraged Jena's mother to get a lawyer?"

Cali answered with no fear, "I advised her to get a lawyer because I couldn't answer her questions and no I don't like changing baby's genders."

He said, "May I ask why?"

Cali explained her feelings; "Just because you change the body, it does not change their minds."

He probed, "So you don't think these kids can grow up and live productive lives?"

Cali answered, "I don't know of any."

He asked, "Well, how is your life?"

She looked at the judge as if to say "is he crazy?" Jena's lawyer objected stating her life had nothing to do with this case. The doctor's lawyer said he would prove her statement would be relevant to the case. The judge allowed him to continue asking questions. He repeated the question to Cali to answer.

She looked nervously at lance, "My life is great."

The lawyer stated, "So, you're saying your life is great but you don't think these kids could grow up and live productive lives?"

Cali frowned at him; looking at him as if to say "what are you talking about?" She looked from him to Jena's attorney back to the judge. Her blood was pounding in her ears.

He said with a check-mate kind of smile, "What would you say if I told you were West Woods Hospital's first infant sex change?"

Color drained from her face as she wished the floor would just open up and take her away. "What did you just say?"

He repeated, louder this time, "I said, you were West Wood's Hospitals first baby sex change.

Jena's lawyer had objected and the judge threw the question out but the damage was done. Cali looked for Lance and only thing she saw was the door closing. She ran off the stand to try and catch up to him. He was sitting in the lobby on the bench with a dead stare. Cali reached to touch him on the arm; he looked at her and said, "I guess we now know what your dream meant."

Cali sadly called his name as if to say I didn't know about this. "Lance."

He walked away without saying a word. His heart was too broken to say anything at the moment. She watched the love of her life leave her. Cali now knew they had lost their case and in the process wanted to destroy her. She went back inside the court room and asked Jena's lawyer to put her back on the stand; she wanted everyone to know about the real Cali. He asked her if she was sure.

She replied with tear drenched eyes, "What more could it hurt at this point?"

The judge allowed her back on the stand. She mustered the courage and told them of her life, she began by say. You know, as she looked down at the suit she had on, a couple of years ago the only thing I felt comfortable in was a pair of boys sweat pants. Yelp that all I wanted to put on. I would leave out the house wearing a girl outfit, and once I got to school I would change to boy's clothing. Everything I did pertained to being a boy. I cried every night because I felt like I was in the wrong body. I couldn't talk to anyone, not even my parents, because they had separated. Cali looked up in the air and said, "Mom now I know the big secret".   Dr. Martin put his head down in knowing, what Cali was referring to. She went on to say. A good friend helped me to come to terms with myself. She showed me how to dress, how to walk, and even how to talk. Cali shook her head as she membered." I can't thank her enough for those countless hour of talking me out of killing myself." I even went to college to take up psychology so I could better understand myself. After final excepting who I was, I met a wonderful man and finally let my guard down and married him, this man had the right to know who he was marrying , so now you have the true life of Cali Evans Roberts and once again you have destroyed it as she looked at dr. martin. Pointing her finger accusingly at Dr. Martin, "You had that man marry another man! I hope he would someday forgive me!"

Cali walked dejectedly out of the court room. Almost all of the lady jurors were crying, even the stenographer. Cali went home to try and talk to Lance and admit to him that was the reason she was getting tested and how it was just too big to tell him, but when she got there he was not there. She listened to the messages on the answering machine, but none of them were from Lance. There was one from Dr. Owen; she heard him say he needed to talk with her as soon as possible. Cali erased the message saying to herself, "I already know."

She grabbed a suit case and packed her things. She looked at her wedding picture and kissed it good-bye. She didn't feel right taking it with her. The only picture she took was the picture of Meghan. She took off her wedding ring laid it on the table along with her credit cards he gave her and her bank card; she wanted nothing from him. She went to her office and looked around; pulling back the drapes to see the view she would never see again. And then she sat at her big high back office chair and spun around for a second. Cali smiled, but she knew the life she once had would never be the same. She didn't know where she was going or what she would do now that she knew she was born a man; she only knew she had to leave the city before Meghan came back. She didn't want her to try and talk her out of it and there was no reason to contact her parents because she now knew their big secret.

Cali got up from her chair and put her new license on the desk. She figured she no longer needed it. She closed the drapes and took one last look around at the office and closed the door leaving the keys in an envelope underneath the mat. She did want to leave a letter, she knew there were no more words to say. She didn't even take the Mercedes Lance bought her; she left in her Honda. She stopped by the gas station and even filled up a five gallon can with gas. As she rode off she could see the city she used to call home grow smaller in her rear view window.

Cali was driving by an open field; she saw nothing but mountains and a sign that read "five miles to Arizona." She did not want to be found and didn't want to have anything to remind her of her former sham of a life. She drove herself into the desert away from the highway, got out of her car, took all of her belongings and started pouring the gas around and in her car. She cried until she had nothing left. She lit a match and set it on fire. She watched the fire grow and along with it her memories. Finally, she picked up her remaining luggage and walked away, never looking back. She was in good shape so five miles was no problem for her; she walked and stared off into the horizon; the sun was just beginning to set.

Chapter 26

After driving around listlessly, Lance checked into a hotel and ordered a bottle of whiskey. He removed his jacket, his tie, and sat in the living room quarters of his suite. He poured a glass and drank it straight down. He didn't want his soberness to linger; he went straight for the gusto with another stiff shot. He sat and thought about what was said in court and could not believe he did not know Cali was a man. He paced the floor trying to think how he could have missed something like that. Just to think the only woman he'd ever loved turned out to be a man. He knew he could never return to his job because the news media would be all over it knowing he was a prominent Doctor of a hospital. Lance poured himself another glass of whiskey and he started to think about all the conversations he had with Cali. She'd never pursued him, he pursued her, and he now knew why she never wanted to date, she wasn't really attracted to men. He remembered her waking up in a panic about that dream and rationalized out loud as the alcohol began to take effect, "If she would have known what that dream really meant she would have never shared that with me." He even thought back to the times she complained about how her mother was always forcing her to go see Dr. Martin and she didn't know why. "She had never given herself to anyone but me and then when she finally finds out what was wrong with her, she had to find out the way she did."

Lance jumped up out of his chair and screamed to the walls, "Oh my God! Cali never knew she was a man! She couldn't have known. She was being haunted; that's why she told me she wished she would have checked something out before we got married. And here I was telling her she could tell me anything." Lance picked up the phone and dialed his house but there was no answer. He grabbed his jacket and said aloud, "I think I know where she probably is." He headed for her office, a bit too inebriated to drive but he took the chance anyway thinking she would be there like she had been the other night. When he got there he knocked on the door calling her name, but got no answer. He remembered the spare key underneath the mat. He lifted it up to get it and found all of the keys were under there; that meant that Cali had no keys. Lance went inside anyway just to check but found the office feeling cold as if it were abandoned even though it was fully furnished. He went into her office where her desk was and that's where he noticed she had left her licenses.

Lance left to go home; when he got there he opened the door shouting for Cali, walking through every room hoping he would find her in one of them. Returning to the bedroom, he seen Cali's wedding ring along with all of the credit cards that he had given her. All of her clothes were gone. Lance went to the garage; her Mercedes was there; she had taken her old car. Lance's worst fears had happened Cali was gone. He went into the kitchen and poured himself another drink and sat down at the kitchen table. He tried to reach her by her cell phone but it was already disconnected. He could not believe just in a couple of hours his whole life was shattered and she removed herself from him like she never existed. Recovering from this would be hard; he didn't want to think of recovery at the moment; he wanted his life back. He wanted to love his Cali again.

He went to take a shower and as the water ran down his face he closed his eyes envisioning seeing his Cali, he felt her lips on his, he felt her making love to him. His heartache was too much to bear; he crumbled to the shower floor crying out for Cali.

*****

Cali arrived in Arizona and checked into a motel under a different name. She was tired from her walk and not as in shape as she thought. All she wanted was to just get to her room and take a shower. She made her way to her favorite escape; she truly believed they helped her get rid of negative thoughts or stress she was feeling, but this shower was different. It was all good although she was trying to erase all the good times she shared with her friend Meghan. Her thoughts veered to Lance and the first time they made love, their wedding, and them laughing on the beach. Her chest heaved; she thought she was all cried out. But the more she allowed her memories to play out the more the pain took a hold of her. She remembered him coming home to work to make sure she was okay and how he was always concerned about her well-being. She thought sadly the shower wasn't doing the trick that time. It only reminded her of all of the love she was leaving, Cali cried in the shower calling for Lance and Meghan, she was all alone in a place that didn't know her and had no love for her. Lance and Cali had no idea that even though they were miles apart, they both still felt the bond of their love as they cried at the same time for each other.

The next day Lance hired a private investigator; he wanted Cali found. He wasn't sure if she left the city or not; he couldn't see her leaving Megan but he couldn't be sure since Megan was now married. He figured she wouldn't want to burden her, that's just how Cali was. He gave the investigator the make and model of the car she was driving and prayed she hadn't done anything drastic.

Cali went to the motel manager to see if there was a library around. She told her it was down the road next to the YMCA. Cali asked her was it in walking distance. She told her it would be about three miles. Cali didn't know if she had it in her to walk again that day. She asked where she could buy a car; the manager said that everything was up in that area. She knew she would have to walk but she would be driving back. The motel clerk asked Cali if she wanted her to call a cab. She thankfully said, "That would be great I should of asked you that first."

The bubbly and helpful clerk made a quick call and turned back to Cali letting her know he should be there in about forty-five minutes.

Cali smiled her thanks, "That's perfect." Cali went back to her room to get her purse. When the cab got there Cali had him to take her straight to a car dealership. She didn't want anything fancy; she had to conserve her money. She had no idea how long she would have to be unemployed and she didn't even know if she wanted to practice psychology anymore. She had a lot to think about and decide on what she wanted to do with the rest of her life. The purchase was nice and quick; she felt good to have a car again. She knew keeping the Honda she would have been traced right away, but what if Lance wasn't looking for her anyway? The she would have destroyed a perfectly good car. But this way she could believe he was looking for her but couldn't locate her because she no longer had that car.

The thought made her feel better that someone could be looking for her in this world. After she bought the car she made another necessary purchase; a lap top computer. This brought her somehow a sense of connection since she no longer had a phone and besides it would save her time from running back and forth to the library. Cali also picked up enough food to last her a couple of days.

Lance got a call from the investigator telling him he needed to talk with him about some information he found out. He was excited to here word about Cali. The investigator told Lance that Cali's car was found burned five miles outside of the state line of Arizona. Lance looked as if he was hit with a ten ton boulder. He was afraid to ask, "What are you telling me? She's dead?"

He explained, "Not for sure, but the good news is the police didn't find a body."

Lance looked confused, "Well what could have happened to her? I don't understand. I had that car checked out; it was in good condition. Maybe someone saw her driving alone and ran her off of the road and look I can't think the worst I got to believe Cali is alright. I think I would feel it if something serious had happened to her."

The investigator said, "Yeah, that's what we need for you to do; think positive. She's an adult and we have a better chance finding a missing adult than a missing child. I have some leads and I will be getting back to you in a couple of days."

Lance begged, "Please, if you get any kind of news let me know. And thank you for all of your help so far."

*****

Megan knew Cali was supposed to find out about her test. She was worried about her friend and tried calling her cell phone, but didn't get an answer. She nervously called her at home with fear in her heart; she felt something was horribly wrong.

Lance answered the phone, "Cali?"

"No Lance, this is Meghan."

Lance immediately began asking questions; "Have you heard from Cali?"

"No, that's why I'm calling to speak with her." Meghan pulled her feet out of Doug's hands as she sat up. "Lance you sound funny; did something happen?"

He sounded so sad, "Meghan I can't go through this over the phone. But I will say Cali's gone. I don't know where she could be."

Meghan was getting upset, "She's gone? She's gone where Lance?"

Lance fought back a sob, "I don't know. Meghan I've looked everywhere for her. I've hired a private investigator to help find her too."

Megan said, "I'm staying at the Hawaii Select Hotel in Hawaii. Please, please call me if you hear anything. Lance I need to know something before you go, did she leave because of something she had to talk with you about today?"

Lance answered, "No she didn't have a chance; it was brought up in court."

Meghan was mad for her friend at finding out in such a way. "Brought up in court? By who?"

Lance answered tersely, "Apparently Dr. Martin was Cali's doctor when she was born. Shall I say more?"

"Oooooh my god, what she must be going through right now. I know this was a shock to you too. Did you two get to talk about this at all?"

Seems like he was about to get into this over the phone whether he wanted to or not. "No, we didn't get a chance to talk, when I heard that she wasn't ah, I just bolted out of there. I didn't expect to hear something like this. I thought she was going to tell me something like she couldn't have kids. I didn't expect to hear she was really a man. Megan you just don't hear shit like that, I'm sorry. I just want to talk to her."

Meghan was surprised to hear this, "You still want to talk to her?"

Lance couldn't stop his tears, "Meghan, I still love her. I don't know how to deal with this yet. I don't see a man when I think of Cali; I just see my wife. You know the funny part of this was I told her she could count on me and that she could tell me anything, but when it happened I just left her to face all of those people probably looking at her like some science experiment gone bad. I left her Meghan. And now she's gone and I am more worried because she didn't even call and tell you where she was going." Lance had another call on the other line he told Meghan he needed to answer it. Before hanging up she reminded him to call her if he heard anything. He promised he would and clicked over to the other line.

Doug was standing by Megan as she was talking to Lance. He didn't know what they were talking about but he gathered Cali was missing. When she hung up Meghan reached out for Doug and cried, "Cali's gone."

Doug tried to comfort her, "She'll be back, try not to worry."

He held her tight as she said, "I hope so honey. I sure hope so."

Doug had no clue how serious all of this was and Meghan couldn't tell him. She'd never spoken to anyone about Cali's secrets so she wasn't about to start; even if he was her husband.

*****

Lance answered his call that was waiting; it was the private investigator telling him he had located Cali and wanted to know how he wanted him to handle it. He thought a moment before telling him he wanted him to give her a letter he would write; at least she would know what he was thinking at the time and how he felt now. The investigator asked him when he wanted him to pick it up. He told him he would have it ready by that next morning and then he asked him if he thought she would still be in the same place. The investigator stated he had someone watching her and would know if she went anywhere.

Lance said, "I don't want her spooked if she catches someone following her."

The investigator reassured him, "It's a woman watching her so she won't expect a thing. My agent's room is next to hers."

Lance felt somewhat relieved, "That's good. Okay, I'll see you tomorrow."

Lance was so nervous it was like meeting Cali for the first time. He stayed up all night to write the letter to Cali being careful he didn't miss anything he was trying to say to her.

Dear Cali, please know I loved and still loves you. I apologize for leaving you the way I did after always telling you how you could talk to me about anything. "I don't care what you were". I only know you as Cali and that's all I see and know of you. Meghan called and she is worried about you too. Please call her as soon as you can. She said she and Doug are staying at the Hawaii Select Hotel. Cali let me say again, I don't care what you are. I just know you made me happy and I think now we know I won't be in the dark about anything in our relationship and when you come home we can go back to the Bahamas where we can start a new life. I guess that's why you were told you don't act the same as other women and I hope you're not taking offence to that comment, but that was one of the things I loved about you. I know I've broken my other promise to you when I told you, you could talk to me about anything but I won't break this one I promise to take care of you. I know you are out there all by yourself and I don't want you to worry about cash so I am enclosing a check for ten million dollars; your still married to a billionaire. Cali, I told you what was mine; was yours and this promise I will keep. You can do what you want with the check. I am just hoping that you will come home to me and forgive me for not being there for you and if you decide you don't want to come home then I hope the money will help you start over. Make no mistake, I love you. I want you to please come home,

Love, Lance

He sealed the letter and sat quietly for a moment; he just felt so hopeless. He had not talked with Cali and had no clue as to what state of mind she was in because this affected her life in more ways than one.

The next morning the investigator picked up the letter from Lance. He himself was clueless of the contents of the letter, even the fact that he was dealing with a billionaire. The investigator gave the letter to his agent and instructed her not to speak to Cali; just hand over the letter.

The agent knocked on the door. Cali asked, "Who is it?"

She thought maybe housekeeping needed to pass out fresh towels, but the agent said, "It's your next door neighbor."

Cali had seen the lady next door and felt she was harmless enough; she thought maybe she wanted to borrow some sugar or something. She cracked the door open and the agent handed Cali the letter. She took it and instantly saw it was from Lance. She moved to open the door to ask the lady where did she get the letter from but she was gone. When the housekeeper made her rounds a bit later, she asked where was the lady that was in the room next to her and the housekeeper told her she'd checked out this morning and that she'd just missed her as she pointed to her driving away.

Cali went into her room and shut the door making sure to bolt it. She closed the blinds. It wasn't that she thought Lance would hurt her but it was scary how fast someone could track you down if they really wanted to. Burning her car did nothing. Someone was still able to track her down in two days. Cali sat the letter on the dresser thinking it was divorce papers he wanted her to sign. She paced around the room looking at the letter, speculating its contents. She mumbled to herself, "Boy that sure was fast, but I forgot when you have money you can do anything. Well I'll sign his divorce papers and get this over with. I'm glad to get on with my life." She sat down on the bed where she could see herself in the mirror and asked herself, "What life? What life do I have?" She was terrified of that letter. She stood up and paced the room again; she kept walking around looking at it everything except opening it. She didn't know what to do.

She suddenly decided to take a shower as she always did when any form of stress came along. This time she washed her hair; she knew she would be ready to open that letter once she calmed down. She put on some comfortable clothes and even made herself a sandwich and then got the letter off of the dresser. She settled onto the bed comfortably to take her time to read it. When she opened it a piece of paper fell to the floor. She picked it up and turned it over; it was a check for ten million dollars. Cali thought that she would have a heart attack. She looked at it again to ensure she wasn't seeing a mirage with the numbers. She unfolded the paper to read the letter that accompany the check; it was from Lance telling her he still loved her and that he wanted her to come home. Cali knew he still loved her and this only confirmed it. She also knew she would never find another man to love her the way Lance did and she didn't want to. It was now clear what she should do. The next morning Cali packed her things. She'd never felt better or more alive, she felt that God had given her a second chance and she was going to take it. As she drove she felt the wind beneath her feet.

Lance could not wait to see Cali walk through that door and put their life back together again and they would be off to their home in the Bahamas. It was about three o' clock that afternoon when there was a knock on the door. Lance rushed to open the door. He was happy to welcome Cali home, but it wasn't her. It was a courier giving Lance a letter. He looked at the courier as to say, is this all? Do you have another package for me? Hoping he'd look up and see Cali? Lance took the letter and closed the door. Now he was in fear of reading a letter. He didn't waste any time; he opened the letter Cali started out by saying;

My dearest Lance, you still amaze me with your kindness and your love. When I got your letter I was terrified to read it. I waited hours before I got the nerves to read it. I thought you were sending me divorce papers to sign or a letter telling me you hated me but when I got your letter you gave me life. I had left to find a place to die; I am a man in a woman's body. How many men would want to be with me knowing this? And this time I know the truth about myself. So I cannot lie, when you sent me that letter I'd never felt so loved. You wanted me back and you didn't care about my circumstances. You are an incredible man and it hurts me to know that someday some woman will have you as her husband. I can't bear to think about it. Lance the reason that I did not come back is because I would never want to see the day you look at me as a man. You have taught me how to love and you have showed me what real love is. I have showed you what kind of woman you would be happy with; just make sure she's not a man! Lance you deserve to be happy with a real woman. You deserve to experience fatherhood the way God intended. I hope this experience will never have you second guessing yourself. You are all man! One of the things I'm going to miss is not my husband Lance but my friend Lance, I would never be with you again friend or otherwise. I pray and know God will send you peace about this whole thing and he will send you a wife that you will love even more than me. He will not make us dwell on the fact we made love to a man, but that we once loved someone very deeply. I thank you for the money it was more than kind and it will allow me to be the person I've longed for. So I will say good bye loving you but hoping our paths never cross.

     Take care of yourself, Cali

Lance dropped the letter to the floor as he accepts the fact he had lost his Cali forever.

THREE YEARS LATER

      Lance was glad he had returned to the Bahamas; he had a new practice that was thriving. He was glad to have the hustle and bustle of the city behind him. He knew that Cali wanted him to forget about her but it was the love they felt that kept him happy. Emma doesn't ask him about Cali and he doesn't talk about her. He thought about Cali as someone who died, but left him with fond memories. Lance stood on his porch looking at the sunset remembering this day would have been their third anniversary, but there was something special about this sunset; he felt drawn to it. He began walking towards the sun; he didn't remember ever seeing one so beautiful. Lance rolled his pants legs up and began to walk on the edge of the ocean and that's when he saw this beautiful white overly large Labrador retriever galloping towards him. The dog jumped up on him, he was surprised because he didn't see where the dog had come from. The dog stood almost as tall as Lance and it seemed like the dog knew him. A woman's voice was calling for Calley. As the woman got closer, Lance heard that name again. He realized she was calling for this dog that had jumped him wanting to play. When the lady saw that her dog had paw prints all over Lance, she said, "I am so sorry that she jumped all over you like that. She has never done that before. I will be more than happy to have your clothes cleaned for you."

      Lance said, "I heard you calling for her. What is her name again?"

      The woman answered, "Calley, Lance smiles as he looked up to the sky, as if to say is this fate. She was given to me by my father when I moved here to be my protector. And by the way my name is Jessica. I feel it's safe to tell you since my dog took a liking to you."

      Lance was enjoying her accent and wanted to hear her say more, "You have an accent, where are you from?"

Jessica smiled as she noticed how handsome he was, "London. I moved to New York to go to school and then I moved here so I could have peace with my writing."

Lance nodded appreciatively, "Oh, you're a writer. That's awesome. This is a beautiful place to write and create."

Jessica stated proudly, "Yes, now that you know all about me and my dog, what is your name?"

"I'm sorry it's Lance. I've lived on this island most of my life off and on. I just moved back here three years ago to set up my practice."

She asked, "Practice? What is it you do?"

Lance said, "I am a doctor."

It was her turn to nod with appreciation; she said, "That's great! I am sure the island can always use more doctors."

Lance smiled and said, "I sure hope so."

Jessica tucked her fingers firmly around her dog's collar, "Well it was nice meeting you. Maybe I'll see you around. Sometimes I need to get Calley's daily walk in as well as mine."

Lance petted the dog on her head, "Yeah, sure, see you around."

Jessica tugged gently and called for Calley, "Come on girl, let's finish our walk." But Calley didn't seem to want to leave Lance's side. Jessica called to Calley again but Calley was confused because she wanted Lance to come. Jessica was surprised; she had never seen Calley act that way since she had raised her from a puppy. Lance hunched his shoulder as to say, "I haven't a clue." Jessica called to her dog once more and Calley tugged at Lance's shirt for him to come along too.

Jessica said, "Well I guess we're not going to walk unless you come too Lance."

"Okay, for the sake of Calley." He started walking alongside them. They both laughed. On their walk they ran into a stand selling ice cream. Lance bought Jessica and Calley a cone. Jessica was surprised at Calley's behavior towards Lance, but Lance knew it was his Cali letting him know that Jessica was the woman for him. They enjoyed their walk on the beach and their dinner that night and by the end of the day Jessica and Lance both knew it was fate that brought them together and they would be together forever.

SEVEN YEARS LATER

Meghan had just come in from the pool and following closely behind on her heels were her two children, little Doug who was six years old and her daughter Casey, four years old. Meghan had to dry them off and put them into some dry clothes, herself included. Big Doug was watching the game and asking what time was dinner. Megan chided with him to keep his knickers on and made her way towards the kitchen to get dinner ready. She noticed a letter on the dining room table addressed to her. She had to speak loudly to be heard over his game, "Hey Doug! When did this letter come in?"

He belched and took a swig of beer before answering, "The other day babe, I thought you would've seen it by now."

She laughed, as she thought to herself, "Only my man."

She went back into the kitchen to fix his favorite meal, spaghetti and meatballs, which also happened to be the kid's favorite. She'd even perfected his mother's recipe over the years that had everyone looking forward to this dish every time she announced they were having it.

After the kids finished eating Meghan had the nanny get the children and wash them up for bed. Even though she had a housekeeper's she still liked cooking for her family; she just let someone else clean up. Megan was removing her apron when she remembered the letter was still in her pocket. She sat down and opened it up. A picture fluttered to the floor. When Meghan picked it up; it was a picture of a man, a woman, and a child; neither of whom looked familiar to her. She sat the picture down and began to read the letter.

Dear Meghan, a lot of years have gone by and I have started a new life. When I started out on my journey I had to completely erase my past; that included everyone I have ever known and loved but no one was as hard as leaving my best friend; a person that had shown nothing but love and friendship when there was no one to be found. A person that would give up going out on dates just to make sure her friend was okay.

As Megan read the letter she figured out who it was from; it was Cali. The tears began to pour from Meghan's eyes; she thought she would never hear from her friend again. She had missed Cali more than she would ever know. She continued reading the letter.

Meghan, the turmoil of not feeling like a woman out-weighed me being a woman. I've thought of coming home and continuing my life as a woman, but now that I know I was born a man I want to live out my life the way God made me. I had the operation to return me back to a man. I knew that even as a man I wouldn't be able to have children but I've adopted a son and am now married. I've taken the name Kevin Mason. I travel around speaking on this type of surgery and encourage doctors to look for alternative solutions so no other children will have to live through what I did. At my next speaking engagement I want you to come and meet your new brother. Megan picked up the picture again and looked at her friend; all these years of suffering and now he's at peace.

THE FINAL ENCOUNTER

Kevin had a book signing in New York and the turnout was great. He had just finished and was taking the elevators to the lobby with some of his book fans.   As the elevator reached the ground floor Kevin was about to exit when he recognized a familiar face. It was Lance with his new wife Jessica. Both looked well and happy.

By sheer coincident Lance was there for a Medical conference. Kevin had the advantage of knowing Lance, but lance didn't recognize Kevin because of his change. Kevin quickly put on his sun glasses to further conceal anything that may look like Cali. He traveled along with the crowed as they exited the elevator, but even that could not hide the chemistry he and Lance once shared, because as Kevin past, Lance turned around to look at him as though he knew who he was. Kevin felt Lance's piercing eyes on his back, but he dare not turn around, because Lance would know it was him. Lance stared as the elevator doors began to close with a slight sadness. Did you know him, His wife asked? Lance replied, as he cleared his throat and tried to gather his composure I thought I did. Kevin knew that even though they had once loved this was the way it was meant to be, as he smile and finally walk out of Lance's life forever.